The Missing Sapphire of Zangrabar

A Patricia Fisher Mystery

Book 1

Steve Higgs

Dedication

To Teresa Daw for her inspiration.

This book came about when the lady who works the reception at my office asked how I come up with ideas for my stories. Paused on my way out the door, I spent the next five minutes inventing a main character, giving her an event that would cause change in her life and throwing in a curve ball that would become a story arc.

The idea simmered for six months and grew in its potential until I just had to write it. The adventures you are about to read could never have been if lovely Teresa hadn't asked that question.

To say that this changed my life would be a massive understatement. Just a few months after publishing this book, I quit that job and have been writing full time ever since.

Table of Contents:

Prologue: New York Geological Society

A shadow moved across a window high above the street. It moved surreptitiously, doing its best to blend into the background, and vanished into the darkness again on the other side as if it had never been there at all.

Only one set of eyes saw the shape sneaking along the side of the New York Geological Society and they belonged to a cat.

The cat, a pedigree Burmese called Sausage, watched from the couch in her owner's fifth floor apartment across the street. Sausage blinked, tilted her head slightly, and chose to deal with an itch on her derriere rather than pay any further attention to what might be going on across the street.

The shadow was joined by a second as its accomplice sidled along the thin ledge.

'The street is quiet,' remarked the second shadow, feeling nervous now that they were almost there.

'You think we should have done this during the day?' asked the first shadow with a chuckle. He knew his partner hated his constant jokes and how he never seemed to take anything seriously, but what was the point of breaking into impossible places and stealing their priceless stuff, if you didn't have some fun doing it?

Before his partner could start griping, or tell him to knock off the humour, he gripped the edge of the window frame they left unlocked three hours ago.

This was the kind of job he'd been dreaming about his entire life. A single job that would net him a score big enough to retire on. He wanted to do this by himself but there was no way to pull the job off without a partner.

Fortunately, the schmuck he sought out to help him had no idea what the sapphire was worth. He would give him a cut sure enough but was going to lie through his teeth about how much he sold it for. Not that he had a buyer yet, but that was a concern for tomorrow, a thing to worry about once he had the jewel.

Weeks of planning, watching the building and the staff to establish patterns and find a weakness was all going to pay off. This was going to be it – the big score.

With his partner keeping watch, he slid the pry bar from his pack and gently levered the window open.

Had Sausage been watching, she would have seen the two dark shadows appear once more only to vanish instantly as they jumped through the open window to drop down to the floor on the other side.

The accomplice checked the time on his brand-new digital watch. Not that he'd bought it, of course. Slight of hand to relieve people of their belongings was a skill he'd learned and then developed when he was still measuring his age in single figures.

Digital watches were the new thing. He could impress a girl just by wearing his.

Cupping a hand around its face to prevent the bright red liquid crystal display giving their position away, he noted the time. It was the start point for their excursion.

They had a ten-minute window. That was how long it would be before the guards came around on their next patrol.

Ahead of him, his partner was hustling to get to the stairs, and he needed to jog to catch up. This was going to be the big one. That's what his partner insisted. All they had to do was get the giant jewel and get out.

Mostly I was dumbfounded. At myself that is. How had I not known? How had I not seen any signs? They tried to deny it, but it was all too obvious.

My husband was sleeping with my best friend.

Even thinking the sentence in my head was too much to bear. I was driving on autopilot and going far too fast. A blast of horn as I whipped around a corner and nearly took off the front of a van as it crept cautiously from a junction, broke my unpleasant reverie.

I sniffed loudly and gulped back the awful pain in my throat. I wanted to cry and howl and wail, but the tears wouldn't come yet; I was still too stunned. As I slowed my car to a pace more likely to ensure I arrived at my destination in one piece, I replayed the scene in my head.

A diary mix up on my part was what caused today's revelation. How long would their affair have gone on if serendipity hadn't intervened? I thought Maggie and I were getting our hair done today. I didn't yet know if I was right or she was, but she clearly had a different day planned; one which involved having sex with my husband.

Maggie and I attended school together many years ago, meeting on our very first day and we had been firm friends ever since. Our lives diverged as adults when we pursued different paths, but I met Charlie when I was nineteen and that curtailed any thoughts of a career of my own. In contrast, Maggie had moved to the city and made her fortune, landing a job in publishing which turned into a great career, and then a business to run when she opened her own firm at thirty-nine. Now she worked mostly from home, going to the office maybe once a week to oversee what was happening.

Her own husbands - there had been three - all left her, and she hadn't visibly grieved about any of them. She just opened a bottle of wine with a shrug each time and kept moving. She always was a bit of a man-eater, but I had never imagined she was capable of such treachery.

Charlie went to work this morning or, at least, that was the ruse I fell for. As he went out the door, I received my perfunctory kiss on the cheek then settled in front of the TV to watch last night's *Dancing on Ice* final. My hair appointment with Maggie was listed in my diary at eleven o'clock so at half past ten I swiped on a dab of makeup to hide the bags under my eyes - bags that appeared literally the morning after my fiftieth birthday - then snagged my keys from the hook by the door and left the house.

Maggie lived in the next village just a couple of miles away. We both grew up in East Malling, a small and old village in Kent in the southeast corner of England, and I still lived there. However, Maggie swapped her houses like her husbands, each time moving into a bigger and swankier place. She now owned a six-bedroom oast house on the outskirts of sister village West Malling. Goodness knows why she wanted so much space, it was huge for one person, but I suppose it wasn't as if she had to clean it; she had a cleaner for that and a gardener for the garden and an odd-job man to boot.

It was almost laughable that when I pulled onto her expansive driveway, my first thought was that the car parked next to her house was an exact duplicate of my husband's. It was only once I was out of the car that my brain caught up with me: It was Charlie's car.

Even then, my innocent brain told me that the two of them must be colluding on something for my birthday in two weeks' time.

Silly Patricia.

I didn't want to spoil whatever surprise they were planning, but I was super curious to discover what they might be up to. At the front door, I rang the bell and waited. I had to ring it again before it was answered, but it wasn't Maggie at the door, or my husband, Charlie. It was her cleaner, a young woman whose name I could not remember. She looked like a mum with young kids in need of an income that fitted around school hours. She had a duster and cloth in one hand and wore yellow marigold gloves that contrasted almost violently with her all-black leggings, baggy t-shirt and trainers outfit. I was a cleaner myself, a job I had started twenty years ago when my dreams of having children had been finally and irrevocably dashed. It wasn't a glamorous job, but I got to keep my own hours, I was my own boss, and I sort of liked peeking into other people's lives.

The young lady was looking at me expectantly, 'Hello,' I said. 'I'm Patricia, Maggie's friend. She's expecting me.'

The woman just nodded her head and moved away from the door so I could come in and shut it behind me. She had headphones on, the kind that go right over the ear that are popular again now, and I could hear the music coming from them though I couldn't make out what it was. It was clear that speaking to her was pointless unless I shouted.

As she drifted away, I put my bag down and called out, 'Maggie. We are going to be late.'

She was somewhere in the house, but while it was large, it wasn't so vast that my voice wouldn't carry to wherever she was. I kept quiet about Charlie being here. If they were planning a surprise for me, I didn't want to ruin it, so I played along, pretending that I hadn't seen his car.

'Maggie,' I called again when I got no response, but then I heard movement upstairs. It sounded hurried, flustered, and the first tendrils of doubt crept into my head.

Why would they be upstairs?

Curious, I walked through the house to the foot of her winding spiral staircase. It was at the back of the house inside one of the two oast towers. By the time I arrived, I could hear Maggie on the landing above me.

'Maggie?' I called out. 'What's going on?'

Looking up, I saw her face as she came down the stairs. Her hair was a mess, and she was wearing a dressing gown. Her eyes were wide with panic, at least that's what I took it for.

'Maggie?' I prompted again when she didn't answer.

'Patricia what are you doing here?' she asked. Now halfway down the stairs, she was still tying her dressing gown around her waist.

Automatically, I said, 'We have a hair appointment.'

She paused to check her mental calendar. 'No, that's next Monday. The eleventh at four o'clock. Don't you remember? We forgot to book it and that was the soonest she could fit us in.'

I had written the fourth at eleven o'clock by mistake. I shook my head to clear it. 'Where's Charlie?' I demanded, remembering suddenly that my husband was here and not at work. There were a lot of clues lining up and they all carried the same worrying theme.

'Charlie?' she tried to make it sound like my question surprised her. Looking back now, I think she was trying to find a lie that might work, but I was suddenly advancing on her, little mousey Patricia starting to storm up her stairs. 'Charlie, he's ah... he just popped around to...'

She didn't get to finish the sentence because I shoved by her on the wide stair and carried on up to the top floor.

'Charlie,' I yelled, a sense of rage overtaking me. Conflicting emotions telling me I was about to make a giant fool of myself because of course he wasn't here having sex with my friend. There would be a perfectly rational explanation for his presence, and I would look like an idiot while also feeling relieved.

My first assumption had been right though. As I rounded her bedroom door, he was hastily trying to get his belt back through the loops on his trousers. His jacket was on a hanger hanging from the knob of a wardrobe and his shoes were placed side by side neatly beneath it. Not only had he just been having sex with my best friend, it had been going on so long that the passionate fumbling to get each other's clothes off had diminished to the point that they neatly hung their clothes before getting down to it.

I had no words.

Charlie stared at me, his eyes like a rabbit caught in headlights; able to see the onrushing danger but powerless to do anything about it. He was frozen in time, his belt half-on as he waited for me to say something or perhaps racking his brain for the credible lie that might get him off the hook.

Before he could assure me that it wasn't what it looked like, I turned around and left. I was lost, bewildered, confused and even though I was moving my feet, I had no sense of purpose. I passed Maggie in the upper hallway without sparing her a glance and found myself back in my car without noticing how I got from A to B.

I stayed that way, locked inside my own disbelieving head until the horn blast jolted me back to reality. I was nearly home but I had no idea what I was going to do when I got there. Did I open the gin? Maybe. Did I cut up all his clothes and throw them out along with everything else he treasured? Tempting.

Part of my problem was that Maggie was the person I had turned to my entire life whenever I had a problem. I had suffered several miscarriages, the worst one at five months. They were distant memories now, the most recent almost two decades behind me, but it had always been Maggie that I went to. Even back in our school days, it had been Maggie that was my shoulder to cry on over boys or that terrible day when the *Bay City Rollers* split up. Now I had the worst thing I had ever faced, and I had no one to turn to.

I have other friends of course, but not ones that I felt comfortable going to with this. Had it not been Maggie he was cheating with, I would have packed a bag and turned up on her doorstep begging to be taken in. She would have welcomed me with an instruction to stay as long as I needed.

As that thought echoed in my head and I pulled my car onto the driveway of my own house, I realised that I couldn't stay here. I had to get away. It was a small village, and everyone knew me.

The humiliation was one thing, and I didn't want to face it, but I couldn't stay because this was our home. Mine and Charlie's. I stared at it through the windshield of my car now, feeling nothing but revulsion. We had built our home together. Charlie had a good job even when we met. He trained as an accountant and worked in London at a big firm. He was twenty-four when we married and bringing home a great wage. He said at the time we needed to borrow all we could and buy the biggest place we could barely afford rather than play it safe and move again a few years later. He believed the house prices were about to rocket upwards and was proven right not long after we moved in. If we had waited, we might never have afforded it.

Now it represented betrayal. I squeezed my eyes shut, willing the tears to come.

After ten seconds I gave up. All I had was anger and the vaguest hint of an idea.

Cutting up his clothes or breaking his precious record collection wouldn't hurt him. Taking his bank account away would though. Charlie did accountancy work all day long so one might expect that he would do the house finances as well. He refused to though. He always had, complaining that he didn't want to look at books and numbers at home as well. The housekeeping and the money stashed away in savings accounts had always been my responsibility. They were joint accounts, but I doubted Charlie even knew where I kept the passwords for the online login. He might not even know how much was in there.

I nodded grimly to myself as my plan took form, slid from my battered old car, and with a fresh urgency to my stride, I burst through the front door of my house. Seconds later, I powered up my old tower computer and pressed the kettle into service. Then I changed my mind about the cup of tea and went to the drink's cabinet for gin.

I cannot tell you where the calm, dispassionate approach came from, but in the next twenty minutes I packed three suitcases with more than half of the clothes in my wardrobe and threw in a stack of books I had been meaning to read. I stuffed my passport into my back pocket, and once I'd lugged the heavy cases downstairs, I settled back in front of my computer to check all the transfers had gone through.

I was taking it all. A whopping ninety-seven thousand four hundred and twelve pounds and eighteen pence was now stacked high in my current account leaving Charlie without a bean.

The banking apps had kept asking me if I was sure and pointing out that I would get no interest on the funds if I removed them from the high-yield savings accounts, but I steamrolled straight over their advice. I knew what I was doing.

With two fast and strong gin and tonics in me and breakfast a distant memory, I reluctantly acknowledged that a third, while tempting, was not a good idea. There would be plenty of time for gin soon enough.

I was going on a cruise.

Southampton

I had been trying to get Charlie to come on a cruise with me for as long as I could remember. In the beginning, he laughed it off as something we couldn't afford even though we both knew we could. Then he started on the excuses, reasons we shouldn't go such as we might not like the other people on the ship or we might not like the ship, and it wasn't like we could get off once we were at sea. In the end, he admitted that he just didn't like the idea of being on a cruise ship. I wondered then and now if he was secretly hiding a phobia of the ocean or something.

He liked Cornwall.

We went to Cornwall every year, apart from once when I stamped my foot and made him take me to Spain.

However, the planet chose to laugh at my small victory because our week in Spain was awful. The weather was unseasonably hot, a plague of little biting flies descended on our resort, and we both got a tummy bug.

Charlie had willingly held those experiences over me ever since, so we went to Cornwall every year. It isn't that I don't like Cornwall, I love the place. It is quaint and romantic and there are so many forgotten little fishing villages tucked into the cliffs where they have barely changed in hundreds of years.

Despite all that, I knew there was more to the world than the most southwestern county in England. So much more.

I saw it in travel magazines and on TV shows. My friends went away. My father got conscripted into the Army when he was younger, then chose to stay in uniform beyond the two years he was required to serve. In his words, he got to travel the world, and would often regale me with stories of exotic places when I was a little girl.

12

Everyone was getting more from life than me.

I had been accepting my lot for long enough, and now, with no reason to stay and every reason to go, I was on my way to Southampton where the cruise liners all stopped, and I was going to hop on the first one available.

Southampton was little more than an hour from East Malling, which was just long enough for me to calm down and question what I was doing and what had caused my husband to cheat. Was it my fault? Had I caused this?

I had gained a few pounds. That was something I couldn't hide from. At school I had been on the gymnastics team and had continued running for fitness until some point in my thirties when one day I just stopped.

I couldn't say why. It just happened.

Rather than fight back when my waist inevitably began to expand, I bought a larger dress size. There was a vague memory that at the time I had told myself not to worry, I would lose the weight soon enough. But I hadn't, and I had never really tried to.

Now that I thought about it, maybe this was partly my fault. Our love life had tailed off, but that was natural and normal, wasn't it? We had been together for thirty years, surely it was normal that we had sex less often now. But he was having sex without me. Was it because I had allowed myself to get fat and Maggie hadn't?

A speed camera flashed as I whizzed beneath it.

Oh, lord! How fast was I going? A glance at the speedo revealed that I was doing eighty-seven. I was on the A3 passing Waterlooville in my little

Ford Fiesta and I had just been caught speeding. I never went over the limit. If asked, I would have claimed that my car wouldn't do eighty-seven.

What was with that anyway? My husband had a six-figure job and drove a Bentley, but he had argued that when we went out, we went in his car so there was no need for us to own two expensive cars and like a fool I had never put up much of a fight.

Somehow, I had been driving a second hand, worthless car for more than a decade while sitting on bank accounts full of cash. Plus, I made my own money. Was that on me? Or was it on him?

Unintentionally, I was getting angry again. Angry at myself and at Charlie for separate reasons. No matter what, Charlie had no right to cheat on me. That much I was certain of.

My internal back and forth took me all the way to the docks at Southampton where I discovered I had no idea what I needed to do next. Large, billboard-sized signs guided me to the port and there, as I turned one more corner, was a huge ocean liner. Between me and it was a vast carpark filled with cars of every colour and size. The ship was still half a mile away across the slab of tarmac and as I drove toward it, and it filled the view completely, I felt my heart rate quicken. Excitement and anxiety competed to be the dominant emotion driving my pulse.

A steady stream of people were heading toward the ship, toward an entry point at ground level in the centre of the ship's side where the process of filtering down into a line to gain access had created a crowd.

I looked around for somewhere to park and in doing so spotted a glass-fronted portacabin bearing a sign that read 'Ticket Office' on its roof.

There were parking spaces in front of it.

I left everything but my handbag in the car as nervously, I pushed the ticket officer door open. Inside, the portacabin was a plush office with two immaculate and prim looking ladies in a purple uniform with dusty yellow neck scarves.

'Good morning,' one said. 'Are you looking for an upgrade? Or to book your next trip?'

'Not exactly,' I said, feeling so nervous that I had to check the ground to make sure my feet were still in contact with it. My pulse was hammering in my head to create a din that threatened to block out all other noise. This was daft. What was I doing?

The lady who already spoke indicated the seats in front of the desk she was sat behind.

'Please take a seat. Marie and I will be able to help with your enquiry.'

Wondering if I should bolt, I convinced my feet to cross the six feet to the chair.

'Can I get you a drink?' Marie asked, getting up as I sat down.

I stared at her for a bewildered second.

'Err, yes please.' My mouth was dry from the gin I knocked back an hour ago.

Marie walked a few feet to where a coffee machine sat on a table. It was one of those that could dispense anything from tea to coffee to hot chocolate and more.

'A coffee, please. Two sugars,' I said when she paused by the machine, waiting for my decision.

'One coffee, two sugars coming up.' There was a happy bounce to her voice, like she loved her job and getting coffee was the best part of it.

'Now, what can we do for you?' asked the lady who had first addressed me. I glanced at her name badge where I read 'Bianca' in bold letters. It was like an out of body experience. I knew I was there in the ticket office, but my brain felt detached from my body.

'I want to buy a ticket for a cruise,' I said with as much casual confidence as I could muster. Could a person even buy a ticket at the port? Was that a thing?

Marie set a coaster in front of me and placed a small, white porcelain cup on top of it. I thanked her but didn't pick it up for fear I would rattle and spill it. I was feeling foolish and exposed and that was heightening my nerves.

'What sort of cruise interests you?' Bianca asked as she swivelled a computer screen to show me some of the many options. 'We have packages in all price ranges. Our Caribbean cruises are extremely popular as are our shorter excursions to Scandinavia. Have you sailed with us before?'

I gulped. It was time to go for broke. With a slight tremble in my hand, I pointed out of the window. 'I want to go on that one.'

There was no mistaking what my arm was pointing at. The ship filled everything in view.

Bianca risked a glance at her colleague, her eyes flaring with surprise. 'That ship leaves in just a few hours.' It was a no, but a cleverly disguised one.

I couldn't allow them to put me off.

'That's perfect,' I managed to croak despite the terrified, parched desert my mouth had become.

Bianca chewed her bottom lip, just for a second.

'I can check if there are any available rooms if you would like me to.' She didn't sigh at the futility of her task, but her tone sounded like one anyway.

'Yes, please.' I breathed a silent sigh of relief that she hadn't instantly said it wasn't possible, but now I worried that there might not be any rooms left. Surely such a massive vessel couldn't be one hundred percent full?

As Bianca tapped some keys, Maria picked up the questions, 'Where is it that you are hoping to go? This vessel is the Aurelia. Its first stop is Madeira and then it travels on to St Kitts in the Caribbean. A lot of people will fly home from there of course but it will travel onward to America, stopping at Miami and New York before...'

Bianca cut over the top of her, 'I'm afraid there are no rooms available, Mrs...'

'Fisher. Patricia Fisher. Really? No rooms at all?' Surely that had to be a mistake. 'I really need to get away.' Even I could hear the pleading in my voice. I hadn't thought this through at all, I just reacted and now I worried I might have to go home again.

Where else could I go?

'The only room available is one of the upper deck royal suites,' Bianca explained. Her tone made it abundantly clear that she knew the room was available all along but knew, just by looking, that I could not afford it. She hadn't said the words, but I was feeling uppity about it, nevertheless.

17

'How much is it, please?' I asked.

'Oh, err. That depends on which cruise you wish to take.' Bianca was surprised that I had asked and was now looking at the screen again, no doubt looking for a figure that would shock me. 'Our shortest cruise ...'

'I want around the world.' It came out more forceful and determined than I expected. I never spoke to people like that.

Bianca flicked her eyes up from the screen to see if I was serious, caught sight of my annoyed expression, and flaring her eyebrows, turned her head to find the number I would need.

I was going to pay for the royal suite and go around the world in style. How dare she think I couldn't afford it?

'The three-month around the world cruise, starting and ending in Southampton and staying in the royal suite is ...' Bianca locked eyes with me, perhaps wanting to see how I reacted to the number.

I asked her to repeat what she had said.

Could she see the blind panic in my eyes? She looked away again, reading from the screen to ensure she made no mistake.

I swallowed hard. It felt like trying to take down a melon in one gulp.

Still waiting for me to respond, Bianca added, 'Of course, that comes with over two thousand pounds worth of on-board spending money, and all your meals are complimentary. Like other passengers, you have free classes and entertainment, plus many other benefits the lower-class passengers do not have access to.'

Oh, well that's okay then.

The sum was more money than I could afford to pay. It was everything I had. If I did this, there would be nothing left for me to start a new life when I returned.

'And there are no other rooms?' I begged. There had to be another room. There just had to be.

'I'm afraid not, Mrs Fisher. This is our largest, newest, and most popular ship and this is the most popular time of year for cruises.'

'When is the next ship that does have space for me?' I asked, my voice now barely more than a whisper; the confidence of a few minutes ago, now long forgotten.

Another mouse click. 'Next Tuesday, the Anubis docks. I can check that for you if you like.' Bianca and Marie were both maintaining their professional politeness, engaging with the crazy woman, and trying to help her.

I picked up my handbag from the floor by my chair. I couldn't wait here until next week.

'Thank you,' I mumbled as I floated out of their office, my brain barely connected to my body and operating on autopilot. Okay, it had been a crazy idea, but what did I do now? I got back into my car and turned on the engine but as I pushed the gear stick down and back to engage reverse, I stopped.

What did I do now?

Was I supposed to go home? What then? Patch things up with Charlie? I wasn't ready to see him yet. How could I even look at him? I wanted to cut his wotsits off and mail them to Maggie. But if I didn't get on the ship, what did I do?

I am a fifty-two-year-old, overweight woman with no proper career and a marriage in tatters. I have no children, I have no real friends - the only one I had was sleeping with my husband, and everything I knew, everyone I knew, and everywhere I considered to be home, would remind me of my cheating git of a husband.

I slipped the gear stick back into neutral and turned the engine off again. Yes, it was nuts. Yes, it was all my money and yes it was probably a desperately stupid thing to do, but I was getting on that cruise ship, and I was going to have the time of my life.

With my jaw set and my lips tight, I shoved the door to the portacabin ticket office open once more and stormed in with purposeful strides.

'I'm doing it,' I declared.

Forty minutes later I was heading for the back of the crowd of people funnelling into the ship. I had a suitcase balanced on top of a suitcase that I was dragging behind me and another suitcase that I was kicking along in front of me.

My car was parked surprisingly close to the ship in an area reserved for the royal suites. I placed it between a Maserati and Rolls Royce and then had a fight with the two security chaps there as they assured me the area was reserved for guests staying in the royal suites.

When I produced my ticket, I thought they were going to argue and claim it was counterfeit. I didn't fit the mould. I got that. I had a car worth less than the other passengers' shoes and I didn't look like I had any money at all. Even my suitcases looked cheap – because they were.

They let me pass with a polite look of disbelief and though I suspected they were supposed to carry my luggage or call someone that would, they didn't. As usual, I said nothing and put up with it.

Struggling with the weight of the two suitcases I was dragging, the one I was trying to push along in front chose to fight me every step of the way. It had four little wheels, but one kept digging in, stopping the suitcase in its tracks and threatening to topple it.

Just as I joined the back of the queue, it dug in again. I kicked it once more, but it didn't move. Just a few more feet and I could set my other suitcases down without the people still joining the queue swarming around me to get on board first.

I put my knee against it and shoved. It tipped over forward away from me. Naturally, I lunged to grab it, but the suitcase I had on top of the suitcase I was dragging shot forward with my motion and fell onto my back leg. As that went out from under me the suitcase in front fell over forward with my hand still grasping the handle.

In front of hundreds of bored onlookers, drawn to watch because I was shrieking and yelping, I performed an untidy plié and fell on my backside.

Laughter erupted from the crowd in front and behind me. It wasn't just me they were laughing at though, it was the burst suitcase and the unflattering, oversized, cotton knickers now strewn across the tarmac that caused the most amusement.

Wishing the ground would just swallow me and knowing no one was coming to my aid, I muttered expletives under my breath and started to collect my underwear.

A teenage boy handed me a pink pair of lacy pants.

'Here you go, gran,' he said as he laughed and ducked back to his family. His dad high-fived him as they laughed. The mum knew it wasn't funny but did nothing to berate them as she tried to hide her own mirth.

As I stuffed the last of the offending garments back in my suitcase and wrestled the infernal thing closed, I wondered what God had against me.

When a hand touched my arm, I jolted.

'Are you alright, madam?'

I looked up to find a man in a bright white, spotless uniform with four gold loops around each cuff. He had a matching white hat with a black peak on his head and the shiniest black shoes I had ever seen. He was perhaps fifty, or maybe very late forties and was exceedingly handsome. He was tall too; at least six feet three inches.

'Just a little suitcase trouble,' I explained, trying to hide my sadness with a smile.

Behind the man, half the crowd were still watching me, waiting to see what hilarity I might provide next. Meanwhile the people still streaming from the car park were adding to the crowd of people waiting to funnel onto the boat.

Everyone was looking at me - as if I wasn't uncomfortable enough already. If I didn't get on board and set sail soon, I was going to come to my senses, ask for my money back, and run away.

The handsome man in the white unform saw me glance at the crowd queuing at the door.

'Perhaps I can help you, madam. I'm Alistair Huntley, the captain of this fine vessel and your servant. May I ask, are you travelling alone?'

'Err, yes?' I replied as if I was asking if that was okay. I fumbled for my ticket, but I didn't have to say anything as he reacted as soon as he saw it.

'Madam, our royal guests do not queue to enter the ship.' He turned, raised his hand, and clicked his fingers at two men who were stood doing nothing much near the entrance everyone else was queuing for. They rushed over, clearly subordinate to the man trying to help me. 'Metcalf, Stromberg, take the lady's bags.'

As they collected my suitcases, I noticed that one of the men was much older than the other. His age out of place simply because the very menial task of carrying luggage felt like something a junior member of the crew would perform. Where the younger man looked barely eighteen, the other had to be close to sixty.

They both smiled politely, making eye contact as they took my belongings. The younger man bore the fresh look of youth. Where he shaved, undoubtedly a requirement of the job rather than a necessity, it was clear that his facial hair wasn't really growing yet. The older man had a scar that ran through his left eyebrow and down onto his cheek. His left eye was clear and bright though, so whatever injury had caused the scar hadn't robbed his sight. As they stood with the luggage to await further instruction, I saw his right hand was missing two fingers. The captain asked me, 'May I have the name of your suite, please, madam?'

I had no idea. I stared at my ticket, looking for the line of text that would provide the answer he sought.

When I looked back up, he said, 'If I may, madam,' taking the ticket from my unresisting hand. 'The Windsor Suite. You have exquisite taste, madam. May I escort you to your lodgings?' he asked as he offered me his arm to take.

Goodness. I could get used to this.

I looped my arm through his and we left the rude boy and his father and all the other riffraff behind. Captain Alistair Huntley escorted me to a private door hidden beneath an awning not fifty feet from where the crowd were still queuing.

As we walked, the captain engaged me in polite conversation. 'Madam, as captain, may I personally welcome you aboard Aurelia, the world's largest ocean liner. Aurelia was launched in March 2017 right here in Southampton by Queen Elizabeth herself. She was built in Belfast by Reilly Shipping and took three years to construct. The interior fit was completed in South Africa and took a further nine months. To keep it stable they had to make the ship very wide. It is one hundred and two feet wide which means the Aurelia can only just fit through the Panama

Canal, as it is just one hundred and five feet at its narrowest point. About thirty feet of the ship sits beneath the water, which is a small percentage of the ship's overall height. There are twenty decks, fourteen of which are for the passengers. The bottom six house the two thousand five hundred crew, provide storage space for fuel, food, and other provisions, plus the ship's mighty engines. Aurelia is one thousand three hundred and twelve feet long. For comparison, the infamous RMS Titanic, was eight hundred and eighty-three feet long. In terms of space available, the Aurelia is nearly five times larger than the Titanic.'

While he was talking, and I was looking about trying to take in as much as I could, we boarded an elevator. I expected stairs, but Captain Huntley had just told me that the ship was twenty stories high. Of course, there were elevators. There were probably escalators as well in some of the open areas.

One thing was clear, I was going to need a map. As it travelled upward, the music playing quietly in the background changed. I had never consciously noticed lift music before but when the new track came on it was *Lady in Red* by *Chris De Burgh*. The stoic façade I was clinging to started to crack. Charlie and I had danced to this at our wedding. It was the song he had picked for our first dance. He said it reminded him of the night we met.

The elevator pinged, and the doors swished silently open to allow bright sunlight from outside to flood in. We were now high above the land outside, my view uninterrupted, save for some glass, all the way over Southampton and the South Downs and beyond. I couldn't focus on it; my eyes were filling with unwelcome tears.

The captain was still talking but had finished telling me about the ship he proudly captained.

'One final word of caution, madam. We have recently suffered several thefts from passengers staying in our best suites. Jewellery mostly. I can assure you we have our best men on it, but please make sure your priceless and most sensitive belongings are securely locked away in the room's safe.'

I almost laughed at the concept: I didn't have priceless jewellery. But the laugh choked in my throat. I was giddy from all that was bombarding my senses. The captain of the ship was treating me like royalty. Given the price passengers staying in the top deck suites had to pay, it came as no great surprise, but I doubted many get escorted to the suites by the captain himself. It was all too much.

The song proved to be the final straw. It struck home what had happened to me today. I was a spurned woman; my husband giving his affections to another. The captain's steady arm was the thing keeping me upright as the emotion of the day threatened to overwhelm me, but even that couldn't stop the tears as they finally broke through the flood gate and began to run down my face.

'Here we are, madam,' said Captain Huntley proudly as he stopped me in front of a large door marked with the title 'Windsor Suite' at eye height. As he let go my arm and reached for the door, I looked up at him with tears silently streaming down my cheeks and he saw the mess I had become.

His eyes widening in a brief flutter of panic and confusion.

'Is everything alright, madam?' he begged to know.

The door to my suite was open and he was guiding me inside. My luggage was already stacked neatly on a low table clearly designed for unpacking. However, as I took in my palatial surroundings and tried to answer his question, that was when I elected to dissolve completely.

'No,' I sobbed, the words came out distorted as I began bawling. Captain Huntley was trying to free himself of me - no doubt he had other duties to attend to. However, he was the rock I was clinging to, metaphorically and physically as I wrapped him into a hug and leaked saline onto the pristine white cotton of his uniform. 'My husband cheated on me,' I managed between heaving sobs.

Another person entered the room – I heard their soft footsteps on the carpet behind me. The captain gesticulated rather than speaking, his arms imploring the new person for help no doubt. I felt sorry for the man, but I couldn't let him go for fear I would plummet into a chasm of grief I would never climb out of by myself.

A gentle hand touched my arm - the new person wanted my attention. My eyes were squeezed tightly shut, but I opened them to see who it was. A young man with Caribbean features and a kindly face looked back at me and I wondered how mental I must look. I had the poor captain locked in a bear hug, my arms around his back to hold on while his hands and arms were trying not to touch me. He was leaning away from me as I was leaning into him.

'Sorry,' I sobbed. I let Captain Huntley go, almost collapsing when my legs disagreed with the request to support me. The young Caribbean man caught me, a gentle arm going around my waist.

'Let's settle you on the bed, madam,' he said, his tone soothing. Out of place with his features, his voice carried a perfect English upper-class accent.

In the distance I heard the captain's voice, 'Madam, I'm afraid I have other duties to attend to. I must leave now, but I leave you in the very capable hands of your butler, Jermaine. He will see to all of your needs.'

I blinked through the tears as I looked at the captain's face, 'Butler?'

27

He was hovering by the open door to my suite; his desire to depart obvious and unsurprising.

'Of course, madam, all our royal suites have a live-in butler in an adjoining cabin.' He apologised again, then escaped while he could.

I didn't blame him, but the embarrassment I felt only added to the crushing burden of negative emotions engulfing me. I turned to the younger man, knowing that I looked a fright but unable to do anything about it.

In the next minute, he helped me onto the bed where I continued to bawl wordlessly while he closed curtains and turned on table lamps to make the room dark but not black. Then the young man knelt at the side of the bed and took my hand.

'Now, madam, why don't you tell Jermaine all about it and let's see if we can't work this out together.'

I let my gaze find his face. It was fixed with an encouraging smile that made me want to trust him. On a random Tuesday in June, on board the world's largest ocean liner in their most fabulous suite, I poured out my heart to a total stranger. I cried, and I cried, and I cried, my throat aching from the effort of it, and eventually, I slept.

Exploring

I slept fitfully that afternoon until a violent dream I instantly forgot caused me to wake as I thrashed against an imagined force.

Beside my bed was a pitcher of water; condensation running down it told me it was cold. I sat up and poured a glass. It was refreshing but it wasn't what I wanted. Now that I was awake, all the misery of my life was back, and I wanted to drown it with alcohol.

I needed to get up, not least because I needed the bathroom. I was hungry also, but in wondering where I could find a restaurant and what food they might serve, I remembered that I had a butler. The very concept made the earth tilt beneath my feet.

I had a butler. His sole job was to make my life a pleasure.

My suite consisted of eight rooms and was bigger than my house. Jermaine's quarters were an annex to my kitchen so that he was never far away and always available.

For more than an hour before fatigue swept me into oblivion, Jermaine held my hand as I talked and sobbed and sobbed and talked. He proved to be a great listener and told me to, "Not be shedding no tears for no man," somehow delivering a colloquial sentence in his upper-crust voice. I knew he was right, but once the tears started flowing, it had been hard to switch them off.

I cringed at the memory of blurting out my thoughts to him as if we were old friends. Telling the poor man how my husband and I hardly ever had sex anymore and when we did it was clear he wasn't excited at the prospect. I told him about Maggie and her trim waist compared to mine and lamented about how I really needed to lose weight on this trip so I could win him back. We even arrived at the vulgar subject of how much money I had just spent on this silly, ridiculously expensive and indulgent room.

'Don't you worry, madam,' he had soothed me, 'all these things can be corrected.' Jermaine explained that we were stopping at Madeira in two days and in St Kitts three days after that. I could disembark at either place but was more likely to find a flight from St Kitts since I had barely any time to arrange one from Madeira.

I could fly home and I would be given a partial refund that would be equivalent to roughly ninety percent of the amount I had spent, less the cost of my initial five days. It was a huge relief. Jermaine also promised to introduce me to his friend Barbie who was a physical training instructor in the upper-deck gym. She would help me shed a few pounds while I was on board if that was truly what I wanted.

Jermaine made it all sound so easy.

While I was undoubtedly snoring like a warthog, my butler unpacked and ironed my clothes, organised my jewellery, and made the suitcases disappear. During my stay he would ensure my room was kept clean, he would bring me whatever I needed, and act as my guide if I wanted. Anything I needed him to do, probably up to and including wiping my bottom, was in his job description.

At some point while I was sleeping, the ship had set sail. I could feel a faint vibration in my feet when I forced myself off the bed.

Staring at the view outside my windows, I huffed a hard breath and promised to get my life in order. I was on this ship now and there was no option to get off for the next couple of days. I would turn things around, arrange to get off at Madeira or St Kitts and fly home. There I would find Charlie full of apology and we would talk things through. I still couldn't decide if I shared the blame for his infidelity - had I driven him to it?

Whatever the case – it was too much to figure out my feelings on the matter right now - I was his wife, and we would find our way through it. In the meantime, I would eat sensibly and lose a fraction of the unwelcome weight around my middle.

The haggard woman looking back at me from the bathroom mirror was not a welcome sight. No one should have to look at that. It was another thing I was going to have to fix. I didn't exactly have a lot of money left from buying the cruise ticket, but there was enough to cover the cost of some makeup and a few clothes.

An hour later, I had bathed and dressed and done my best to find an outfit choice that didn't make me look like I was going to the supermarket. I was getting hungry as I hadn't eaten since breakfast some eleven hours ago.

A fruit bowl in the kitchen provided a banana to stop the audible rumbling coming from my belly, and as I munched on that I made promises to myself about what I was going to eat and drink. It was a luxury cruise ship so they would have all manner of food on offer. Somewhere, there would be something healthy for me to eat here. Perhaps some poached fish or a salad would suit my needs.

Though I was slightly concerned I would lose myself and need to find a guide to get back to my suite, I set off to find a bar and restaurant. It didn't take long. The moment I stepped outside the delicious aroma of exquisite food assailed my nostrils. My stomach gave a meaningful growl.

'Can I help you, madam?' asked a man in a purple uniform. He wore the same dusty yellow around his neck as Bianca and Marie in the ticket office, but his was a tie. He was spotless and immaculate just like all the other crew I'd seen so far.

'I'm looking for a restaurant?' I answered, making my reply a question.

31

He smiled in return, 'Follow me please.'

He led me around a corner and along a wide passageway. The distant sound of chatter filling the air grew louder as we neared a mighty pair of ornate double doors. They opened automatically I thought but passing through them I discovered a pair of young men holding them open. This place was so swanky they had two men employed just to open and close the doors.

'Would you like to be seated for dinner now, madam, or will you be taking a drink at the bar first?'

We were heading toward a man that I took to be the Maître d'. He was dressed in … I didn't know what it was called but he looked like he should be serving food at Downton Abbey. His white jacket ended near his knees at the back in what I think are called tails.

I gulped. I felt so out of place. I was convinced that everyone was looking at me, judging me and wondering what I was doing in their exclusive club. However, when I worked up the courage to look about the room, I saw no eyes on me. Even so, it did little to calm the rising unrest I felt.

'I think a drink might be necessary,' I croaked, my voice coming out as little more than a whisper.

'Very good, madam,' he replied. As we passed by the Maître d', my guide quickly introduced him as Frederick and explained to him that I was the guest staying in the Windsor Suite. He didn't slow his pace, but I caught an appreciative nod from the man as if the name of my cabin meant something.

Across the restaurant, we arrived at the bar and once again I had to swallow hard as I took in how grand it was. All the men were wearing suits and ties, all the ladies were in cocktail dresses, and I was the plainest person in the room. I wasn't the only person without a partner though. Directly in front of me was an old man. He was sitting on a bar stool with his thin legs dangling. He peered down his nose at a cocktail menu, struggling with his bi-focals perhaps. Beyond him a pretty girl in her early twenties waited patiently for his order and beyond her was a range of gins that would rival anywhere on the planet.

Finally, I felt at home.

'I'll leave you with Vanessa,' my escort said. 'When you are ready to eat, just let her know and Frederick will come to you.'

'Thank you,' I replied, my eyes mostly on the bottles behind the bar.

He said, 'Have a good evening, madam.'

I turned to say something in reply, but he was already gone, weaving his way back through the room. He'd spent no more than two minutes by my side but in that time managed to make me feel like royalty, just like all the other members of crew had so far.

As I took the seat next to the old man, he looked up at me.

'Good evening,' he said. He was looking over the top of his glasses now, smiling at me politely. He might be eighty years old - it was hard to tell, but he had the slightly withered look that many people get as they age. Fading away gracefully, his suit had a neat waistcoat and a chain that led from one pocket to the button in the middle and then to the pocket on the other side where I assumed I would find a watch. He still had hair on his scalp, mostly white and a bit wispy, but it was combed neatly to the right in a style he might have been keeping for fifty years or more.

'Hello,' I replied with a smile of my own. 'Do you mind if I join you?'

He smiled up at me in confusion for a moment, his attention then swinging to the left as his elderly wife appeared by my shoulder. Wordlessly, he stood up and went with her arm in arm to their table, never giving me a second glance. Glumly, I settled onto the nearest bar stool.

I glanced down at my hand where I had taken off my rings and dumped them in my purse - my left hand looked odd without the trio of engagement, wedding, and eternity rings. I had worn them for so many years. Their absence left an obvious band of pale and smooth skin.

It sent a skitter of worry through me that I now looked like a cheating wife out to pick up a man for the night. Nothing could be further from the truth.

I locked eyes with the pretty girl behind the bar. 'A gin and tonic please. Make it a double and use the Hendricks gin, please,' my voice came out with steely determination. I might be confused about everything else, but I knew how to drink gin.

My intention to diet could spare me one gin and tonic surely. I was certain I once read that it was the lowest calorie alcoholic beverage. Or one of them at least. Vanessa placed a large bulbous glass in front of me filled with gin, tonic, ice, and cucumber. I took a mighty slug of it, the powerful botanicals crashing into my taste buds in a kaleidoscope of flavour. I gripped the edge of the bar and with my eyes closed I stamped my right foot twice in ecstasy.

Even if the world was filled with cheating men, I could always rely on gin.

Twenty minutes later and lost in silent contemplation, there were three gins in my bloodstream and I was beginning to feel the effects. Sitting at the bar in a funk of my own misery, I was emitting a negative vibe so strong that a space had cleared around me. The two bar stools to my left and right were all empty as those that had approached soon changed their minds and went elsewhere. All the other parts of the bar were filled with patrons.

I knew I needed to get up and get something to eat, but my feet were not responding to the messages I sent them. I would eat (alone), then wander back to my suite (alone) and spend the night in the huge, sumptuous bed (alone) before…

'Would you mind if I joined you?' I turned to find a man standing next to me at the bar. He was hesitating as if unsure which way I would answer or if I were waiting for someone. He was quite handsome and had broad shoulders that gave him a muscular appearance. I estimated his age to be very late fifties, but he had a good head of thick hair, most of which was grey but still retained his natural dark brown colour in places.

I opened and closed my mouth a couple of times as I tried to form a coherent sentence. Finally, I managed to say, 'Okay,' really showing off my dazzling wit.

He signalled for a barperson and settled himself onto the stool next to me. Vanessa arrived, her sweet smile in place. He ordered a beer for himself and before I could protest, he had another gin and tonic placed in front of me.

He thrust his hand out, introducing himself, 'Jack Langley.'

'Patricia Fisher,' I replied, lightly shaking his hand because it would be impolite to not do so. 'Thank you for the drink.'

He held his glass up and waited for me to raise mine. Seeing no way out, I clinked my glass against his as he said, 'Cheers,' with some gusto, 'You're new on board, right? Came on today, yes?'

'Yes.' I was being cautious but now worried I was bordering on rude. Relenting, I added, 'It was a spur of the moment thing. I hadn't really planned it.' Jack appeared to be by himself and perhaps he just wanted some company. He was pleasant not lecherous, not that I had any thought in my head that he might be interested in me, but I decided there was no harm in having a conversation. 'Have you been on board long?' I asked.

'Some months actually. I have become a permanent fixture almost,' he chuckled as if he found it amusing somehow.

'Isn't that expensive?' I asked. My question was reactive, I hadn't thought it through first so only once the words had left my mouth did I realise I was now rudely asking about the man's financial situation.

Thankfully, there was no one else in earshot, except perhaps for one man, another loner, who had positioned himself at a table close by. He seemed to be very deliberately not looking our way and he stood out because he was wearing his sunglasses even though he was indoors. I spotted him the moment he sat down and tried not to stare as he looked over his dark shades to peruse the bar menu.

My attention came back to Jack when he answered my impertinent question. 'Well, I'm a retired jewel thief,' he joked while wiggling his eyebrows at me. 'I'm sure you will have already heard about my antics stealing ladies' jewellery. They seem to be warning everyone as they come on board now. So, with all that, I can afford it. How about you? I was passing the Windsor Suite earlier and saw you going into it being escorted by the captain no less.'

'Yes,' I murmured, rueing the day's decisions. 'Like I said, it was a spur of the moment thing. I hadn't really thought it through. I am planning to get off as soon as I can and fly home.'

'Really? Well, no time to lose then,' he said as he upended his glass. 'You have but a few days to celebrate.'

'Celebrate what?' I asked, the misery in my voice obvious to anyone within ear shot. Then to drive the point home, I snapped out, 'I caught my husband cheating on me with my best friend. I don't have anything to celebrate.'

'On the contrary, my dear,' he countered, raising his hand once more to attract Vanessa. 'You are either newly single, which is something in itself to celebrate, or you are on a voyage of discovery that is undoubtedly long overdue. If you get off at the first stop, will you ever get back on? For the rest of your life you have this one chance to enjoy the absolute luxury of staying in the best room on the biggest ocean liner and all that it has to offer. If you fail to grasp that and wring it for all it is worth, then you will have missed out and the opportunity will be gone.'

His words had some merit to them. The ship *had* set sail. Did I really want to sulk in my room until we arrived in St Kitts?

'Okay,' I mumbled, distracted by the new thoughts beginning to fill my head.

'That's the spirit,' he cheered. Vanessa arrived in front of him. 'A bottle of Bollinger and two glasses, please.'

My eyebrows found their way to the top of my head. I hadn't drunk much champagne in my life – Charlie wasn't the sort to splash out - and Bollinger had always been out of my price range. Also, the gin was taking hold and if I didn't eat soon, I would be drunk.

'I need to eat,' I announced.

Vanessa overheard me while she delivered the champagne and glasses.

'I'll get you a table,' she promised, flicking her eyes upward to spot a waiter or the maître d.

'Great idea,' said Jack as he picked up the bottle in one hand and the glasses in the other. Whether I wanted it or not, I had a dinner companion. He wasn't unpleasant though and Charlie had provided my dinner conversation for thirty years - this might be a refreshing change.

As it turned out, it was. Jack was able to talk with intelligence about the locations the Aurelia would stop, explaining in detail about the amazing places he had discovered. After a while though, I realised he was telling me nothing about himself and any questions I posed were deflected by the same joke about being a jewel thief.

I had already asked how long he had been on board twice, so I tried a different approach and asked how long he planned to continue cruising.

'Forever perhaps. There's no extradition from a ship and I am still wanted in several countries. Even when we dock in America, where they most definitely want to arrest me, I am safe provided I stay on board the ship. Only when I go ashore do I risk incarceration.'

His jewel thief joke had been amusing at the start but was getting old fast. He used it to deflect me constantly. The only personal fact he provided was his place of birth in Brooklyn, New York. His accent would have given it away so perhaps he wasn't telling me anything after all. Then he avoided revealing anything further by asking me questions instead.

The first was the most obvious one to ask since I had already revealed the events that led me to embark on my trip. His prying was done gently though, enquiring whether I wanted to talk about it, rather than directly demanding I spill the beans on the horror of my recent past.

I didn't want to talk about it. Not really. But I couldn't come up with a reason why I shouldn't, so I told him all about my marriage, about my day, and admitted how blind I had been and for how long. I managed to keep my emotions in check, but I sunk another glass of champagne, saw that the bottle was now empty and ordered another bottle.

I was taking Jack's advice and grasping the opportunity before it was gone. I guess I knew that I was getting quite squiffy, but I really didn't care. My room, excuse me, rooms were staggering distance from my current location. I would be able to find my way there or I would flag down one of the lovely crew and have them escort me.

Or perhaps they might carry me.

A carry sounded good.

Jack was asking me something. I was trying to concentrate on his words, but my eyes were getting heavy.

'It looks like we ought to be getting you to bed, Patricia,' his repeated sentence penetrated the fog of my addled brain.

'Hmmm?'

He reached across the table to put his hand on top of mine where it was resting near my champagne glass. I thought for a moment that he was hitting on me but had to dismiss the idea as ridiculous. Why on earth would he?

'You seem a little wobbly, my dear. I shall escort you to your lodgings.'

'That really won't be necessary,' I replied. Or at least that was my intended reply, but my teeth seemed to get in the way when I tried to say necessary, the resulting utterance nothing more than a garbled mess.

I clambered out of my chair anyway using the table for support. Then I spotted the man with the sunglasses again. He was peering at us over the top of a menu just a couple of tables over and tried to pretend he wasn't when he saw me looking at him. His actions were just as odd as his appearance.

I pointed a wobbly arm in his direction. 'Hey, that guy …' I didn't get to finish the sentence because I leaned on the table as my centre of balance shifted and the whole thing flipped over, throwing cutlery, napkins, drinks, and everything else on top of me.

Flailing around to get up and smothered by a tablecloth I couldn't escape, I could hear feet hurrying toward me. The next second there were hands helping me up.

The tablecloth dropped away to reveal Jack and two stewards who had rushed to my aid. He waved them off while doing his best to convince them I needed nothing more than a lie down.

I tried to apologise for the mess, but probably just sounded drunk. All around me, people were staring. Staring and muttering about the ridiculous woman who didn't know her limits. Not that I could hear them, but I didn't need to read lips to know what they had to be saying.

As Jack led me from the restaurant, I glanced back at the bar to find the guy with the sunglasses was gone.

Why had he been watching me?

Missing Jewels

When I woke in the morning, I lifted my head to look about, had a moment of panic when I didn't recognise the room, then remembered where I was, and flopped awkwardly over onto my back.

Like a twist of the knife, the memory of the previous evening flooded back to make me groan at my own stupidity. I had a dry mouth from the over-indulged gin and champagne and a terrible sense of embarrassment. Yet again, there was a pitcher of water on the nightstand. It was just out of arms reach, and the effort required to get to it eluded me.

When had I last been drunk? I couldn't remember. A shock of horror washed through, jolting me into sitting up - I couldn't remember getting back to the cabin! How I did I end up in bed? I lifted the duvet to peer beneath it.

I was in my underwear!

Who the heck put me to bed? Surely Jermaine wouldn't have been so bold. So, it must have been Jack. Had he escorted me to my suite? Dredging my addled brain for snippets of memory, I flashed on an image of him walking me back to the suite with his arm around me for support and then him rooting in my handbag for the door card. I couldn't remember his hands helping me out of my dress but perhaps that was for the best.

I told myself that I must have managed to deal with my clothes without anyone's help and left it at that. I needed to get up though.

Unsure even what the time was - the blinds were shut and the curtains drawn - I slowly twisted my face until I could see the clock beside the bed.

It was just after eight.

I wanted to get up, to get moving, to do something with my day that didn't fall under the banner of feeling miserable for myself. The promise I made to lose some weight and reset my life in the few days that I was away, lasted as long as it took me to meet with my first temptation. Wallowing in self-pity, I put no effort into resisting the drinks behind the bar last night. Worse yet, I overindulged.

How much did I spend last night? I couldn't remember paying. How did it even work on this cruise? It wasn't all-inclusive, it couldn't be with the champagne I had been knocking back last night. A quick check of the contents of my purse would reveal what I had spent.

Angry, I forced myself up, ignored the banging at the back of my head and went to the bathroom. I drank several glasses of water as I picked up the abandoned clothes I found. That my dress and shoes were strewn across the carpet, I took as a good indication I had taken them off myself.

The dress went onto a hanger which I hooked on the front of a wardrobe door. It needed to be laundered but I couldn't find a laundry hamper to put it in. There was a note on my nightstand from Jermaine instructing me to ring for him when I was ready.

Well, I wasn't ready yet.

I needed to feel more human before I dealt with other people, and I had asked him to arrange a session at the gym with his friend, Barbie, this morning. That was going to have to be pushed back a few hours until my hangover subsided.

My phone pinged, the noise like a knife of guilt stabbing directly into my heart. I hadn't looked at it since I fled the house yesterday. It pinged continually with incoming messages during the drive to Southampton, but I chose to ignore it, assuming the texts would be from Charlie.

Reluctantly, I opened my handbag. The screen of the phone was still lit which made it easy to spot. My phone contained no fewer than twenty-seven missed calls and seven text messages. All from Charlie. The first message read:

'We need to talk.'

That was all he wrote, and it was sent just a few minutes after I stormed out of Maggie's house. The next one came more than an hour later when he discovered I was not at home.

'Where are you?'

The rest of his messages were along the same lines. He was sorry I had to find out like that, and he blamed himself for being so awful. I choked when he read his claim to still love me and his hope we could get through this *difficult* time.

The memory of the previous day washed over me like a tidal wave, leaving guilt and sorrow in its wake. What on earth had I been thinking spending so much money on a stupid whim? Charlie would kill me when he found out.

My heart ached at the thought of him. He wasn't perfect, but he was my husband. The only one I thought I would ever need. Should I call him and explain? We would talk about what had happened and ... And what then? I would take him back? I would, wouldn't I?

My brain ached more from the conflicting emotions than it did from my hangover. I wanted to reset the clock and not know about his affair. Or set it back even further and give him no reason to cheat on me in the first place. But then ... how long had it been going on? Had it started while I was still thin? Was my waistline even a factor? Had he been unfaithful with other women besides Maggie?

Once a cheater, always a cheater. Wasn't that what they said? He was to blame here. But ... wasn't I to blame also? I couldn't decide, and I had no one to talk to about it.

Spotting the pale skin on my ring finger, a pang of guilt shot through me once more. I needed to put my rings back on.

Remembering I wanted to check my supply of cash to see what I might have drunkenly spent, I looked about for my purse - my rings were in it, so two birds and all that.

I dug through my handbag but my purse was not where it should be. Perplexed, I questioned what I might have done with it. My rings were in it along with all my credit cards and bank cards and goodness knows what else besides. Had I put my rings in it though? I was more worried about them than the silly bits of plastic that were easily cancelled and replaced. Had I left them in the car? My memory was a bit swiss cheese, but I was sure I remembered seeing them in the purse last night before I set off for dinner.

The next ten minutes was spent rummaging through my bedroom. Becoming exasperated and starting to feel just a little bit sick with worry, I opened drawers I had definitely not opened before. My rings could not be in them, but I checked them anyway because I had already checked everywhere else.

The rings weren't here. Then the answer hit me like a slap to the face.

Jack had taken them along with my purse!

Was it meant to be an extension of the joke about him being a jewel thief? If so, I didn't find it very funny. I pressed the buzzer to summon Jermaine.

'Good morning, madam,' he said through the door less than half a second later. The suddenness combined with his unexpected proximity made me jump clear out of my skin. He wasn't in his quarters as I had imagined but was in the next room waiting for me to request his presence.

'Come in,' I called, one hand on the surface in front of me to support my weight while my heart restarted.

I was dressed in old sports clothing and a pair of running shoes that had never once been employed for running. I didn't remember packing any of it, but Jermaine had laid it out neatly for me to find.

'What can I assist Madam with this morning?' Jermaine asked, standing almost to attention in my doorway.

His presence in my life as my personal butler was too much to take on top of all the other strangeness.

'Jermaine, you know I am not royalty, right?'

'You are to me, madam.'

I sighed. 'Jermaine, I don't need a butler, I need a friend. Someone I can talk to. If you call me madam again, I swear I will scream. My name is Patricia.'

He stared at me, his eyes a little wide while he tried to decide what response to give. I held up an index finger. I had more to say. 'My life turned on its head in the last twenty-four hours. I'm just a simple woman with simple desires. All this,' I indicated around the room, 'is too much for me and it is freaking me out. I'm getting off in St Kitts in five days' time and my only plan between now and then is to relax, lose some of the

45

excess me I have gained, and try to patch things up with my husband if I can. Can you help me with that?'

Jermaine allowed his stiff posture to ease away, his shoulders dropping back and down.

'Yes, mad... Yes, Patricia. It will be my absolute pleasure.'

I nodded my relief. 'Now, I have something of a problem to deal with.' His eyebrows lifted, waiting for me to explain. 'My rings are missing.'

His hand shot to his now open mouth. 'Oh, my goodness!' Until that moment, he had been portraying a stiff, British, Downton Abbey version of a butler from a different era. There had been a trace of effeminateness to his voice, but now that his guard was dropped, the full-gay man emerged, his gesticulations suddenly over the top. 'It's the jewel thief!'

'Yes. I think I met him last night.'

'Oh, my goodness!' he exclaimed again, then his expression changed to quizzical. 'Hold on, how do you know it was the jewel thief you met?' I noticed a change in his accent that I was going to have to ask him about later.

'Because he told me that's who he was. I thought it was just a line to make himself sound dangerous and alluring, but since my purse is missing, I must call that assumption into question. His name, assuming it wasn't fake, is Jack Langley.'

I couldn't tell you what was happening because didn't understand it myself, but I felt different somehow. There was an odd itching sensation at the back of my skull and a sense of purpose was filtering into my bones.

Jermaine was still looking at me in wonder, so I explained a little better.

'I got a little tipsy last night.' Actually, I was three sheets to the wind, a good nautical expression, but Jermaine didn't need to know that. 'He joined me at the bar, plied me with champagne and escorted me back here. I don't remember much of it.' Jermaine's left eyebrow lifted, probably wondering if there was more to tell. 'But this morning my purse is missing, and my wedding rings were in it. They are not worth much. Certainly not worth stealing. However, they are mine and I would like them back. Can you help me find him?'

'Of course, madam.' I twitched but let his failure to use my first name go. 'Even if he gave you a false name, I am sure we can track him down using a description.' He turned and left the room, going back into the living quarters area where he used a telephone on the writing desk to call someone. There was a brief conversation in which he did not reveal why he wanted to find Jack Langley but gave the name and asked if there was a passenger aboard by that name. I could overhear enough that I heard the positive answer and a room number when it was given.

Jermaine thanked the person at the other end and ended the call. 'He is one deck down on the other side of the ship. I know exactly where he is. How sure are you that he took your rings? Could he have been joking when he said he was a jewel thief?' They were both fair questions.

I felt full of indignant purpose right up until Jermaine said we could find him. Now I was faced with having to confront the man from last night, the man that I believed had taken my rings and had been bragging about being a jewel thief.

Was he? Or was I about to make a complete fool of myself?

'Perhaps we can just go and have a look?' I said it as a question.

My butler nodded, deep in thought. 'I feel partly responsible,' he admitted sadly. 'I should have asked you about jewellery yesterday and

47

secured it in the safe. Let's put your other precious items into the safe now, shall we?'

It was my turn to nod, although with a grimace of embarrassment I had to admit that I didn't have anything much of worth with me. There were some diamond earrings that Charlie had given me for our twenty-fifth anniversary and a watch that had some value to it. A few other rings and bracelets that I grabbed as I ran from the house yesterday but that was all. I gathered them up as Jermaine went to an oil painting on the wall in the living area. It was a seascape showing the Aurelia under azure blue skies. It swung outwards to reveal a safe behind it, one with a very solid looking door set flush with the wall. I could see a recessed keyhole and handle. It was like something from an old spy film.

'Where's the key?' Jermaine asked.

I just looked at him. 'What key?'

'The key to the safe. I left it in the door yesterday so that Madam could put her jewellery and other belongings in it. I always leave the door open and the key in it so new occupants can find it easily.'

'I never left the bedroom yesterday until I went out for dinner. I didn't even know there was a safe.'

Jermaine pushed the oil painting back into place. 'This is perplexing.'

'Could he have known where the safe was and taken the key?' I asked.

Jermaine was lost in thought. 'I need to report this,' he murmured, heading for the phone again.

'Shouldn't we check it out first? Maybe ask him if he took my rings and see how he reacts? It's not like he can escape from the ship if he is guilty. Otherwise, we might get other people involved and end up looking silly.'

Jermaine pursed his lips. 'Okay. I think that's a good idea, madam. You don't think he's dangerous, do you?'

It was something I hadn't considered, but mumbled, 'No, I don't think so.' I couldn't articulate why I believed we were safe to approach him. All I could say was that Jack Langley hadn't come across as someone who would kill us both and stash the bodies in a lifeboat. Jermaine was looking at me, I was looking at him, neither one of us quite sure what to do next. 'So... do we go?' I asked.

Jermaine just shrugged. Helpful.

He was six feet and maybe four inches tall and though the immaculate and well-tailored butler's outfit hid his shape, I could still tell he carried a lot of muscle. Wide around the shoulders and thighs, he had the look of someone that could be a member of a SWAT team or a special forces unit. Despite that, he was looking to me for guidance, his comfort zone of butler duties now well behind him. I grabbed my handbag. It didn't go with my sweat suit and trainers, but it was what I had on.

I inclined my head toward the door.

'Let's go.'

With Jermaine in the lead, we easily navigated our way to the cabin Jermaine claimed was Jack's. My butler knew exactly where he was, but I was hopelessly lost. Without Jermaine or a map or maybe some breadcrumbs to find my way back, it might take me a week just to find my suite again the ship was that vast.

Just one deck below mine, the rooms were still opulent and expensive Jermaine explained as we walked. Whoever Jack was, he had some money. Especially if he had been on board for as long as he claimed.

Approaching his cabin, we could both see the door was ajar. Would we catch him leaving and have to confront him in the corridor? Quickening my step, I closed the distance to his door and reached it before anyone came out. Then I slowed and sort of peeked through the gap between door and frame while listening for noise.

'Cooee,' called Jermaine from so close to my ear that it felt that the sound had originated inside my head. I jumped and slapped his arm. 'Sorry,' he whispered. 'I'm a little on edge.'

His call had been loud enough to alert anyone inside the cabin, so I tapped the door and called out myself as I took a tentative step inside the room.

'Hello? Anyone here?'

There was no answer to my call. There never would be. Not from Jack anyway. If I had been chewing gum, this would be the point that it tumbled from my open mouth. In front of me there were cleaning supplies spilled all over the carpet.

Quickly adding the clues, I could picture a member of housekeeping letting themselves into the cabin whereupon they smartly dropped whatever they were carrying the moment they saw Jack's dead body.

It explained the open door, but also suggested that someone was currently alerting other people to the murder. I figured I might as well call it that since I doubted Jack had tripped and stuffed a knife up to the hilt in his own back.

'Psst!' Jermaine was trying to get me to come back out into the passageway where he chose to remain.

I was just inside the door, no more than a pace into the cabin. Rather than obey Jermaine's urgent gesticulations, I moved to the side so he could see around me.

'What is it?' he asked, suddenly curious.

Then his face froze for a split second, his eyes widening in horror as he took in the shocking sight. Acting on impulse, he drew in a sharp breath and was about to scream I felt sure when I lunged to clamp a hand over his mouth.

'Shhhh!' I begged him, locking eyes with the tall Jamaican as I implored that he stay calm.

I had never seen a dead body before, never seen this much blood for that matter, but I was strangely calm. Beside me, Jermaine was all but hyperventilating. I pushed him against the wall in concern that he might faint, patted his arm, and took a few more steps into the room.

It was a big room, or rather it was several rooms - a suite like mine only not so great and not so grand. Jack was laying on the deck in front of a couch, his face turned toward the door, his sightless eyes staring at the way out as if his final thoughts had been of escape. All around him the room was destroyed, and I could see into the bedroom where the contents of the drawers had been upended. The killer had been searching for something.

I just wanted my rings.

'What are you doing in here?' A man's voice demanded from behind me.

I turned slowly toward it, expecting to find someone in uniform and I was not disappointed. There were no fewer than five uniforms crowding the room's entrance - four men and one woman. Peeking around the door was a sixth person who had to be the cleaner. She looked Chinese, middle-aged, and white as a sheet despite her tan skin. The woman in uniform was trying to calm her.

'I asked you a question,' the man repeated, but now that I was facing him, I saw the question was directed at Jermaine, his member of crew, not me, the passenger.

Jermaine's eyes were filled with panic. 'He's my butler,' I announced, fixing the man with what I hoped was a look of confident calm.

Seeing an out, Jermaine took it. 'This is Mrs Fisher, sir. Mrs Fisher is the guest in the Windsor Suite.'

'I met Mr Langley last night. I believe he stole my purse and my rings. He kept telling me he was a jewel thief.' That got their attention. 'But when I came to confront him, this is what we found.' I swept my arm to show the man in charge the scene behind me.

The man wore the same pure-white uniform I saw the captain in. The only difference was the number of gold rings around each cuff – his had only three. I would ask Jermaine later, but I expected to find that he was the second in command or whatever the correct title was for the man that was one below the captain.

He was in his late fifties, with grey hair that was beginning to thin. Standing almost as tall as Jermaine, at maybe six feet and three inches, he towered above me, and he was also broad shouldered and trim around his waist. His accent was distinctly South African.

As I watched, he grabbed Jermaine around his left bicep with a meaty hand. He moved in close to Jermaine's face, making it look like he was going to whisper, then growled, 'Pull yourself together, man. And take Mrs Fisher elsewhere.' Turning to me he made a feeble attempt at putting on a pleasant face. 'Mrs Fisher, I'm afraid this is now a crime scene and under my jurisdiction. You will have to leave.'

Oddly, I found that my feet didn't budge. I was feeling indignant. 'What about my rings?' I asked.

He kept the fake smile in place. 'My team will thoroughly search and catalogue the contents of the room. If Mr Langley is indeed guilty of taking them, you will be informed. Please leave a description of the missing items with your butler.'

Not satisfied, I turned around again to look back at Jack and his trashed cabin. I felt as much as I heard the gruff man cross the room behind me. When he stopped just a foot shy of my back, I looked around and up at his face. He was keeping his anger in check, but I could see it bubbling under the surface.

When he spoke, his tone was stern. 'Now then, madam. I won't have any trouble, will I? I don't want you to turn amateur sleuth on me and ruin my investigation with any poking about you might want to do.'

53

His twitching hands made me wonder if he wanted to remove me by force and then questioned if my status as the guest in the Windsor Suite was the only thing stopping him.

After a moment of reflection, I came to my senses. I don't challenge people – what on earth was I thinking? Mousey little Patricia Fisher says yes and thank you and stays out of the way. It was how I came to drive a clapped-out car while my husband drove a Bentley, and probably the root cause of all the other injustices in my life.

The itchy feeling at the back of my head was still there and becoming more distracting as the man's eyes bored down into mine. Regardless of what was causing it, I needed to get out of Jack Langley's cabin and away from the unpleasant senior cruise ship officer.

There was no reason to stay here anyway. Jack was dead, my rings were missing, and if they were here then I had to hope they would be found and returned to me. I really didn't want to see Charlie without them on.

I strode by the man in charge, who had still not introduced himself, grabbed Jermaine by his wrist, and left the cabin without another word.

The Suspect

Outside in the corridor, I let go a breath I hadn't realised I was holding. Jermaine was right beside me.

'Who was that?' I asked.

'That's the deputy captain, Commander Schooner, madam.' Jermaine checked behind us and ushered me down the corridor a few feet before adding, 'He's a real ball-buster. Most of the crew refer to him as the Captain's Rottweiler.'

Well, I didn't like him. In my head, I acknowledged that I didn't know the man but he stood in contrast to all the other crew members I had interacted with so far in that he had not even attempted to be pleasant. I had to wonder what he might have done if I hadn't left when I did and was glad of my decision to not test him. I could hear him now as he barked orders inside Jack Langley's cabin, the door of which suddenly slammed shut.

'We should go,' advised Jermaine.

I hesitated. 'What about my rings?'

'Do you have a picture of them?' he asked.

'Probably.' I was scouring my head to remember if I had something on my phone I could use.

'If not, a description will have to do. If they are in there, I am sure Commander Schooner will find them.'

'Do you think they will find all the other missing jewellery?' I asked, but I spoke again before Jermaine could, 'Sorry. Silly question. You know as much as I do.' I glanced back down the corridor toward Jack's door and froze. Well, sort of froze, I stopped moving for a heartbeat and grabbed Jermaine's arm to stop him too.

He said, 'Ow,' where I pinched his skin. I shushed him and pushed him into a doorway so we were mostly out of sight. 'Madam, what ...' I shushed him into silence again.

'We are being watched,' I whispered. 'There's a man along the passageway, hiding behind a plant. He was in the restaurant last night by himself and he was watching me then too.'

'Who is he?' Jermaine asked.

I shook my head. 'I think that's something we need to find out. Don't they say the murderer always returns to the scene of the crime?'

Jermaine eyed me with a questioning look. The tilt of his eyebrow made me think he was silently questioning my sanity. It probably didn't help that the man from the bar last night ducked back out of sight the moment I looked his way so Jermaine hadn't even seen him. For all my butler knew, I was making it up.

'I'm not sure if that is a thing, madam. Why would a guilty person ever go near the place that might connect them to their crime?'

Jermaine probably had a point, but the back of my skull was itching again, and I wanted to see if the man followed us.

'Let's head back to my suite,' I said, making myself visible in the passageway once more. I wanted the man to see me. However, as I walked in the opposite direction, giving him every chance to follow me, I had to fight an almost incontrollable urge to see if he was doing so.

Jermaine caught up to say, 'The Windsor Suite is the other way, madam.'

'Then let's take a circuitous route to get there. Whatever you do, don't look, but we need to see if the mystery man is following us. We can do that when we turn a corner.'

'Of course, madam,' Jermaine replied dutifully despite what he was most likely thinking.

We shortly came to a wide atrium, the passageway ending as it emerged into the sunlit area. There were glass panels to our left and right, I guess that should be port and starboard although I couldn't tell you which was which for my life. Glorious blue skies were all around and there was a bustle of people going here and there. A pair of escalators joined this deck with one below it, passengers and crew alike getting on and off ahead of us.

To our left, I spotted a bank of shops. Grabbing Jermaine's hand to make him hurry, I hustled to the nearest open door, swung inside, and found my way to the display window so I could look out and watch for my suspect.

'Can I 'elp madame with anything?' asked a stiff French accent from behind me. I hadn't even looked at what sort of shop we had gone into but since I was now peering outside from between two silk ballgowns, I had to guess it was a fancy boutique dress shop.

'Just, erm, looking, thank you,' I replied, lifting a price tag to inspect it in a fake display of taking interest. The number staring back at me from the tag would have made me spit out my beverage had I been drinking.

'Perhaps madame would be interested in the sale on the next level?' The lady was trying to be polite while also hoping to convince the poorly dressed, plump woman away from her high-end gowns.

I could feel her coming toward me, but Jermaine intercepted her. 'Mrs Fisher is staying in the Windsor Suite.' Apparently, that was all he needed to say. The lady's attitude shifted gear and her voice went from slightly snooty to liquid caramel.

'But of course. Madame must take her time and inspect my fine garments. Please feel free to try anything on. It can all be tailored to fit. We have a twenty-four-hour service, no charge, of course.' She continued to prattle on behind me though I tuned her out to concentrate on the mouth of the passageway. Was he coming or not? Or was it nothing more than my paranoia and imagination that led me to believe the man in the sunglasses was spying on me?

These questions and more cycled through my head until the man from the restaurant last night sidled out into the sunlight. He was trying to be inconspicuous and in so doing was making himself highly visible.

Like last night he wore sunglasses, although to be fair, now that he was out of the passageway and into the sunlight, they were justified. However, the brown Fedora hat and mac, which gave him a Humphrey Bogart-esque look were ridiculously out of place.

It was his movements more than anything though that made him stand out. He darted across the atrium from the point where the passageway terminated until he reached a large plant in a huge pot. Then, from behind it, he pushed two fronds apart to peer through.

Who on earth was he? And what possible reason could he have to follow me?

Not able to spot his quarry from his position inside the plant, he stepped out, finally exposing himself. I got my first good look at the suspicious man.

He was a shade under six feet tall, and disappointingly rather ordinary looking. The hat hid his hair, but the little of it I could see was a bland light brown colour and long enough to curl over his ears. He was a white male in his late thirties, with a touch of stubble showing through where he hadn't shaved this morning. The sunglasses hid his eyes, so I couldn't tell if they were both there or if maybe he had something exciting like a pool ball where the left orb should be. Otherwise, if asked to describe him, there was nothing that stood out. He was average height, average size ... he looked like he ought to be a librarian or an accountant.

Unable to see me as I studied him, he hurried across to the glass balustrade at the edge of the deck so he could check the escalators and the deck below. Whether he saw someone he thought might be me or not I couldn't tell, but he glanced about to see if he was being watched, failed to see me peeking between the display items in the window behind him, and stepped onto the escalator.

'Come on,' I yelled to Jermaine. He was admiring a plum-coloured off-the-shoulder taffeta dress when I grabbed his arm again and yanked him after me. 'He's just gone down the escalator.'

'Isn't that what we want? To lose him?' Jermaine asked, clearly confused by my actions.

'No. I want to know why he is following me.' We got to the escalator, but the man had already reached the bottom. I made Jermaine go in front of me so I could hide behind him but there proved to be no need. The suspicious man didn't look back up. He paused briefly to look around, couldn't see what he was looking for and started walking. Moments later, he merged into the crowd, and I lost sight of him. By the time we got to the next deck down, he was gone.

Standing in the middle of the wide space, with a confused butler hovering next to me, I wriggled my nose and wondered what I was doing. Surely, I should be reporting the man to someone and asking them to investigate his odd behaviour. Instead, I was doing exactly what Commander Schooner warned me not to do: I was amateur sleuthing. Only thing is, I have no idea what I am doing or even where to start. Even though I was thoroughly curious about what had happened to Jack Langley, I couldn't work out what I could do about it. How would I go about the process of snooping around? Would I recognise a clue if I found one?

Frowning at myself, I admitted I was being silly. I was dragging poor Jermaine around on a wild-goose chase for no good reason and he was politely putting up with my antics because he was assigned as my butler.

'Sorry, Jermaine. I'm not usually this crazy.' Jermaine kind of shrugged to say it was fine.

Perplexed by indecision and doubt, I forced myself to focus on something I could do. Last night I swore I would find a gym and shed a few pounds while I was on this trip. Plus, there were other tasks to which I needed to attend.

Much as I felt drawn to start snooping around, I needed to focus on finding out how to curtail my trip, get my money back, and arrange a flight home.

I also seemed to have skipped breakfast.

On the way back to my suite, I asked Jermaine about the process for curtailing my trip and whether he could help me to arrange a flight home. Of course, he already offered to do exactly that when the subject first came up yesterday.

As my butler he was on hand to meet my every need and that included providing me with a healthy diet, if that was what I truly desired, and arranging physical activity.

I had a lot of conflicting priorities rampaging around my head: win Charlie back, find my wedding rings, work out who the mystery man tailing me is. However, thirty minutes later, as I was standing outside the frosted glass door of the upper deck gym, I put them all on hold. Some exercise as a distraction would be good for me.

That's what I was telling myself anyway. I am such an idiot.

I pushed the door open and peered in.

'Hello,' said a Lycra-clad, size-zero image of female perfection as I cautiously ventured inside. 'Mrs Fisher? Jermaine said I should expect you.'

The woman smiling at me had blonde hair that could have graced the cover of a glossy magazine, sparkling blue eyes, and a deep tan that looked one hundred percent natural. I gauged her age at somewhere just north of twenty, which explained her flawless complexion and the vibrant energy I could feel pulsing outward from her.

She was several inches taller than me at maybe five feet ten or eleven inches – tall for a woman in my book, and if I could place her accent correctly, she hailed from California.

61

'Hello,' I replied nervously. I was willing my feet to move forward, but they seemed quite reluctant. I had been a gymnast until my twenties and distinctly remembered having a thin waist at the time. It was a distant memory though, the hours of honing and stretching so far in the past that they might just as well have never happened. 'Are you, Barbie?'

'Yes,' she replied brightly, then saw my hesitation and came to get me. I had a brief thought of escape but missed my chance as she was taking my hand and leading me in.

'So, what is it I can help you with, Patty? Would you like some general fitness exercises to perform or would you like to transform yourself while you are on board? I understand you have booked the around the world cruise. Three months is enough time to transform your body or find your inner strength. You set the goals; I am just here to help you realise them.'

Barbie had a permanent smile, just like the doll. It was beguiling somehow, and I fell under her spell. I meant to say that I was planning to get off at the next opportunity, but my lips betrayed me. Before I knew what I was saying, I was bragging about being a gymnast a *few* years ago and signing up to get fit.

She squealed and clapped her hands in excitement before snatching up a clip board with a form for me to fill in. I signed it wondering if it was actually a waiver so the cruise line couldn't be sued after I had a heart attack in the gym.

'I'm so happy,' Barbie said. 'We are going to become so close. Is it okay if I call you Patty? I just know we are going to have the best time. I love helping people find their inner strength. Okay, let's go!' Her brain seemed to be wired directly into the mains. It was hopping from one thought to the next, her sentences coming out in a torrent. She led me from the gym's reception area into a side room that had a scale on the floor and a chart on the wall, plus an odd-looking device that reminded me of the set of dividers I used to have in my school geometry set. These were twenty times the size though.

'First we need to establish our baseline to work from,' said the gorgeous stick-insect as she ushered me onto the scales.

If I could have come up with a reason why I couldn't be weighed I would have, but my brain wouldn't fire, so I stepped unhappily onto the device half expecting it to yell, "One at a time," as I did. I glanced at Miss Perfect, but all she did was look at the number the scale displayed and tap the tablet in her hands to note it. She then took a tape measure and noted the girth of my hips, chest, thighs, and arms and then picked up the giant dividers.

'What are they?' I asked.

'Callipers,' she answered while failing to explain, but as she advanced, it was obvious they were to be used to measure the excess on my belly. A final entry on the tablet and she set it down before bringing her face up to mine. 'Ready?' It was a rhetorical question though, as she then grabbed my hand and all but bounced through the next frosted glass door and into the gym itself, which from henceforth will be known as Igor's Dungeon of Pain.

Barbie took me through some stretches, warming me up gently she said, then put me on a treadmill with a slight incline to walk for five minutes. After two minutes I was sweating profusely and out of breath.

Barbie came over to check on me. 'Okay, I think you are warm now. Shall we get started?'

'Started? I think I'm okay for today. I don't want to push myself too hard too soon.'

This was the point when I realised my mistake.

Barbie's perfect smile faltered. 'Push yourself?' she squeaked. 'You don't know what pushing yourself is. It's time to get fit, Patty. Let's go!' The last two words were bellowed in my face like a sergeant major to a new recruit.

Terrified and confused by her blend of encouragement and rage, I spent the next hour jumping, running, getting up, getting down, lifting weights, trying to not die, and all with the undivided guidance of my very own personal torturer, I mean trainer.

I kept trying to stop because I needed a rest. Each time she would say, 'Is that how you get fit? Is that how you get your figure back? Does resting burn calories? I don't think so. Get moving!'

Just when I thought I might pass out, she said, 'Well done, Patty. That's it for this session.' I stared her dead in the eyes because I thought for a moment that it was a cruel trick of some kind. It wasn't though. The session was over, and I had survived.

'You did ever so well. How are you feeling?' she asked. I held up a hand to ask for a moment of respite then threw up next to her feet.

'Ewww,' she said as she quickly backed away. 'That's nasty.'

On wobbly legs, I backed away and collapsed. Honestly, I think I might have lost consciousness if I hadn't got my head to the deck first. Looking back, I should have seen the warning signs as the other gym patrons looked horrified when I went into the gym with her. I guess they had seen her in action before. Laying on the mat, sucking in deep, ragged breaths and thankful to still be alive, I decided I didn't really want to be fit and get thin after all. Once I was able to walk and could escape the gym, I wasn't coming back.

Barbie knelt next to me. 'Jermaine said you wanted help with nutrition as well. It's almost lunchtime and after that work out, your body will be craving nutrients. Shall we go to lunch together? I can help you select the right food to aid weight loss and replenish your energy levels.'

'Okay,' I managed weakly. I wanted to get off the mat but didn't have the energy to do it. Willing myself to get up didn't seem to be working. Lifting an arm feebly, I said, 'I might need a hand here.'

Barbie laughed at me. 'You are so funny.' Mercifully, she also stepped in to give me a hand up.

'I … I should help clean that up,' I tried to insist even though I felt like falling over again. Another member of the gym staff was throwing something absorbent and scented over the pool of putrid horror I ejected unwillingly from my body.

'Oh, goodness, no,' said Barbie as she moved to block my path. 'Thank you, Mark,' she said as she motioned to the man dealing with my mess. Then she ushered me toward the door, saying, 'Let's get you cleaned up for lunch, shall we?'

Thirty minutes later I was wearing a breezy summer dress and being escorted to lunch by Barbie, still wearing her impossibly tight Lycra outfit. Her blonde ponytail bobbed along behind her as she tried to explain macro-nutrients and superfoods. It was all gibberish so far as I could tell.

Apparently, she regularly provided the upper-deck passengers with tailored diets that would enable them to get healthy while surrounded by decadent food designed to make them fatter. While other crew were fed elsewhere, she was expected to accompany the passengers to their meals to help them make the right choices. As if shackled to a jailor, we walked by the sweet trolley and took a table for two overlooking the prow of the ship and the pool located there.

With a menu in my hands, my belly gave a meaningful rumble. 'What looks good?' Barbie asked, adding, 'I'm going to have the quinoa, kale, and pomegranate bowl with a bottle of sparkling water. There is nothing better than staying hydrated, don't you think?'

'Um, yes?' I hazarded. 'I guess I'll have the same.' The description of the quinoa bowl was not enticing. I wanted the fresh, line-caught cod steak in champagne batter served on a bed of triple cooked chips. Or perhaps the Wagyu burger. They both looked far more appetising, but I had to acknowledge that neither one would reduce my waistline. Twenty minutes later, in the shower, once my heartrate had finally returned to normal and the sweat was washed away, I questioned whether the session Barbie had put me through had really been that hard. Yes, I had been ready to die for most of it, but could I repeat it? I had survived it once.

'How often would you want me back in the gym?' I asked, trying to keep a light air in my tone as if I was just casually making conversation.

'Oh, that was just a warm up session for me to gauge where your fitness level is. Now we can really start to push you.'

Oh, my God.

'We need to fit in at least two hours a day.'

Oh. My God.

'Just for the first few weeks that is. After that, once your body is getting used to the punishment, we can add a few extra sessions in.'

'I'm getting off as soon as I can,' I blurted.

'Oh,' she said, slightly taken aback. 'I thought you were on the around the world package.'

'I am. I was. I'm not sure,' I admitted. I opened my mouth to tell her why I was on board in the first place, but our food arrived. A white-gloved waiter delivered the dishes on a trolley and served them delicately to our place settings. I'll say this for my healthy plate of bland, it was colourful. It was nothing short of a rainbow in a bowl.

The waiter unfolded a napkin with a flourish and placed it on my lap.

I stared at the bowl of food. It didn't do anything. I looked up at Barbie. Her face was set with an encouraging, if slightly confused, smile. I knew what the foods in my bowl were. I had seen them on menus and watched TV chefs doing things with them. I hadn't ever eaten them though. None of them. I couldn't even spell quinoa.

Tentatively, I put my fork in and took a bite. Across the table, Barbie was tucking into her bowl oblivious to my careful inspection. It was good. Not like a big, fat, juicy burger kind of good, but still tasty and I paused to remind myself that it was healthy stuff. If I had known eating healthy could have tasted like this, I might have tried it years ago.

Between bites, Barbie asked me, 'So what changed your mind about the cruise?' Barbie had no boundaries when it came to topics of conversation.

I didn't have to tell her about Charlie, but I did. It seemed I was telling everyone. Now that I thought about it, who was there that I hadn't told? The captain had been my first victim, then Jermaine, then Jack last night and now Barbie. I was going to have to stop. I needed to get off the pity party, but before I could consider what I needed to do instead, the unwelcome form of Commander Schooner appeared in my peripheral vision. I turned to see what he was doing only to discover he was making a beeline to my table. There was no mistake, he was coming directly at me, and I just barely had time to wonder what he wanted before he arrived, a small entourage of other men in white uniform accompanying him.

He looked at me but didn't speak, then inclined his head to Barbie.

'Leave.'

It was a quietly spoken order that carried no opportunity for discussion. Barbie shot me an apologetic look, dropped her napkin on the table and darted away. She was clearly upset, which made me angry. I might not belong here. I might be the most ridiculous woman ever to sleep in the Windsor Suite, but I paid the money, and I hadn't done it so I could be treated like this.

'Come with me, Mrs Fisher. Let's not make a scene, eh?' he demanded.

'I shall do no such thing until you have explained yourself.' Commander Schooner looked startled. Maybe no one ever stood up to him. Surprised or not, he needed only seconds to recover. Though my pulse was quickening, I refused to flinch away when he bent from the waist to get his face into mine.

'Mrs Fisher. You will be coming with me whether you wish to or not. Now you can cooperate and walk out of the restaurant, or you can resist, and we can carry you out. Which is it to be?'

What on earth was happening? Had Charlie reported the money stolen and tracked me to the cruise ship? Were they going to lock me in the brig or something?

I didn't need to ask though. Seeing the confusion in my face, Commander Schooner held up a clear plastic bag. Inside it was my purse.

'You dropped this in Mr Langley's cabin last night.' He leaned in even closer so that only I could hear him. 'When you murdered him.'

'What?' I shrieked.

Commander Schooner stood back and instructed his men, 'Take her back to her suite.' The four men surrounded me.

'Please, madam,' one of them implored, not overly happy about the prospect of wrestling a middle-aged woman from the upper-deck restaurant. I complied, standing, and allowing them to walk me back to my suite. I was in a daze though and barely conscious of the people looking at me as we passed.

How had I gotten to this point?

'You will be handed over to the authorities in St Kitts,' Commander Schooner explained. I was sitting in one of the high-backed chairs in my suite, lost and confused and struggling to make sense of the ground shifting beneath my feet. 'The evidence against you is compelling ...'

'What evidence?' I asked, interrupting his flow.

He stopped his pacing to stare at me, an amused smile playing across his lips. 'You were seen leaving the restaurant with Mr Langley last night. Your belongings were found in his room which proves you lied about not seeing him after he dropped you off here, and you were found in his apartment earlier today trying to disguise the evidence.'

'None of that is true!' I cried, horrified that anyone could believe I was capable of such devious intentions. Then, reviewing my denial, I added, 'Well, apart from the bit about leaving the restaurant,' I admitted, 'That part's true, but I was too drunk to have gone anywhere apart from to bed by myself.' My heart was thumping in my chest.

'Inebriation is not hard to fake, madam,' Commander Schooner shot back. 'It is my task to keep the passengers on this ship safe and part of that task is to deal with crime. I never thought I would have to deal with a murder,' he shook his head when he said the words, his voice dripping with disappointment. 'You will be confined to your rather palatial suite until we reach St Kitts. There will be a guard outside, so don't try to leave, Mrs Fisher.'

He turned to go but I called after him, 'Wait,' I begged, desperate to make him see what a mistake he was making. 'Wait, there was a man last night in the restaurant. He was watching me. He had on dark sunglasses to hide his eyes and a coat with the collar turned up. I saw him again today outside Jack's room. He's been following me. He must have something to do with this.'

Commander Schooner flipped his eyebrows, looking around to share the joke with the members of the ship's security team filling my suite. 'Really? A mysterious man in a coat and a pair of dark sunglasses. Like the ridiculous made up story you hastily concocted about looking for your rings. Please don't waste my time and insult my intelligence, Mrs Fisher. You have been caught. The decent thing is to accept it.' With that he crossed the room with the rest of the guards on his heels. They filed outside, the last one closing the door behind him.

A single tear escaped to run down my left cheek. I swiped at it angrily. I was innocent, so there was nothing to worry about, right? The police would investigate, and they would clear my name and find the real killer. Would they though? How hard would they look? Commander Schooner thought the evidence against me was compelling. Those were his words, and I knew I had no alibi to confirm my whereabouts at any point after I left the bar last night.

Would they just lock me up for a few months while I waited for a trial, and only then allow me to plead my innocence?

I needed Charlie. I needed a lawyer and I needed Charlie. I took my phone from my bag and called his number. As I heard it ring at the other end, I began getting nervous. Would he even answer? What did I say to him when he did?

'Patricia? Is that you?' It was him. It was Charlie. I wanted to be able to have him put his arms around me and make me feel secure. But did I really? He had cheated on me, and I didn't know where that left us. From one moment to the next, as my emotions fought with each other, I found myself unable to decide if I wanted to hold him tight or kick him in the wotsits. Mostly, it was both.

'Charlie,' I managed to stammer in reply.

'Patricia tell me where you are, and I will come to get you. I'm sorry, Patricia, I truly am. Just let me come to get you.'

'I'm on a cruise ship,' I admitted meekly.

There was a confused pause at the other end, after which he said, 'What?'

'I'm on a cruise ship,' I repeated. 'We sailed from Southampton yesterday. I am halfway to Madeira already.'

'But ...' He was going to ask a question when a new one occurred to him. 'How did you pay for that?'

'Don't worry,' I said as I sniffed back tears. 'I will be getting off in Madeira if I can and will fly straight home.'

'Madeira,' he echoed, 'I don't believe this. What on earth are you doing on your way to Madeira, you silly woman?'

Hold on. Why was he questioning me? Why was he calling me names when I should be the one shouting at him? I didn't get a chance to answer though as my door opened without a knock to precede it and Commander Schooner swept in again with a team of men. 'Search everywhere,' he instructed them. 'Let me know if she attempts to intervene.'

My anger went from nought to sixty in a heartbeat and I was speaking through gritted teeth when I said, 'Charlie, I have to go. I will call you back shortly.' I hung up the phone and stood up. I'm only five feet six inches but my rising rage was making me feel much taller than that as I crossed the room to get into Schooner's face. Almost toe to toe with him, while a shocked crew watched, I poked him in the chest. 'Just what is it that you are going to say to me when I am proven innocent, Commander Schooner? Hmmm?' I got no response as if the concept were unthinkable. 'I appear to be staying in the best suite on the entire ship and you are treating me as if I have smuggled aboard and deserve not the slightest courtesy. Have you already proven me guilty? Have you?'

The rhetorical question gave him cause to pause. He opened his mouth to speak but I pressed on, cutting over him before he could find a response, 'I find you to be rude, Commander Schooner. My rings were stolen, the story I gave you for my presence in Jack Langley's room was accurate, and once I have cleared my name, I will be coming for yours.' There was a sharp intake of breath from around the room. I was getting carried away and threatening the man in front of me. I really had no idea what I was saying, or where the words were coming from. Meek, mild Patricia was fired up and acting like a princess in a tizzy.

'Very good, Mrs Fisher,' replied Commander Schooner calmly. 'I have not yet proven your guilt in this matter. However, since I think it just a matter of time, you will find me hard-pressed to extract an apology from. My men will be searching your suite for further evidence. I must insist that you stay out of the way while the search is conducted.'

'Perhaps I should speak with the captain,' I raged, my anger fuelled by his calm.

'The captain is well aware of your circumstances. I can assure you he delegates these matters for me to manage, but please feel free to waste his time with a call if you wish.'

I had to fold my top lip over my bottom one to stop myself from swearing. Commander Schooner was an infuriating man. There was to be no arguing with him; I could see the futility of it. Instead, I asked, 'What am I to do about meals if I am confined to my quarters?'

He inclined his head in thought. Then said, 'Your butler is highly trained. He will prepare your meals.'

'What about the use of the gymnasium?'

He looked at me quizzically and I thought for a moment he was going to scoff at my question since I don't look like a gym user. Perhaps he then remembered my lunch companion because he said, 'I will have Miss Berkeley arrange private sessions with you. You will be escorted to and from the gym and have a guard on you while there.'

'Who is Miss Berkeley? Is that Barbie?'

'Yes. Is there anything else?'

'Not yet,' I snapped grumpily as I turned my back on him and stalked to my bedroom.

The men employed to search my suite were making fast work of it and they were being quiet, considerate, and careful. It was rudely intrusive nevertheless, so I was glad when Commander Schooner appeared at my bedroom door five minutes later because I thought he was there to announce they were done. He wasn't though.

'I need the key to your safe, Mrs Fisher.'

'I don't have it,' I replied, boredom in my tone.

'Come now, Mrs Fisher. Failing to cooperate will not help your cause.'

I looked up to meet his eyes. 'Check with my butler,' I snapped. 'I haven't been on board long enough to use the safe. When we looked this morning, the key was gone. Perhaps Jack took it when he was stealing my rings last night. Did you consider that?'

'Very well, Mrs Fisher, you can have it your way. Whatever you are hiding in there will be discovered when we reach St Kitts and I have a locksmith brought on board.'

Now I was mad enough to grit my teeth. 'Get out,' I yelled, looking around the room for something to throw at him.

Still calm, he said, 'Quite the temper you have there, Mrs Fisher. Is that what got Mr Langley killed?'

There was no way to win with this man. My hand was hovering above a vase of flowers, ready to launch it across the room when I found some inner calm and stopped myself. I closed my hand and let it fall to my side. I needed to emulate the calm that he was forcing down my throat. With Jedi-like control, I took a steadying breath with my eyes closed, then opened them and fixed him with a knowing look.

'Your attempts to provoke me are pointless, Commander Schooner. I will have my apology.'

He sniggered at the idea, then turned and walked confidently toward the door. Calling to his men in the main living area of my suite, he said, 'Make sure you disable her internet and confiscate any communications devices. Phone, tablet, anything she can use to communicate with any accomplices.' He moved toward the door, then stopped and spun around to face me again. 'Your passport, Mrs Fisher. Give it to me.'

'I will do no such thing and I don't believe you have the right to confiscate it.' I almost stamped my foot in anger.

'I have it here, sir,' I heard one of the guards report.

I raced from my bedroom, hot on Schooner's heels.

He crossed the room ahead of me and took it from the guard's outstretched hand. I swear he was deliberate in taking his time to inspect it, waiting for my rage to return. When I said and did nothing, seething inside as I bit my tongue, Commander Schooner slipped my passport into a pocket and walked away.

Then he was gone, leaving my suite without another word or even a glance in my direction. The crew he left behind operated efficiently, silently stripping me of my ability to communicate with the outside world. When one of them asked for my phone, I just handed it over. I was angry, but I didn't take it out on him. Soon they were done and began moving toward the exit. The man who took my phone paused in the doorway to say someone would be back to disable the internet shortly and then I was alone in my suite, surrounded by palatial opulence and trapped like a common criminal.

I felt an almost overwhelming need to lay on the bed and cry. So much had happened to me in the last twenty-four hours. Doing so wouldn't get me anywhere, but I was more alone now than I ever had been in my life, and even though I was completely innocent, I might still be in a lot of trouble. What if no one believed my version of events? I had to face the very real fact that I might need to find my own way out of this.

How did I do that though?

Fighting tears and a sense of desperate helplessness, I swung myself into the seat at the writing desk and grabbed the mouse for the computer. Nothing happened until I found the power switch, and while I waited for the screen to boot up, I grabbed a handy pad of paper to begin scribbling notes.

What did I know?

Not a lot was the answer but that was an unhelpful approach.

'Come on, Patricia,' I psyched myself up and wrote, "mystery man," in the middle of the page. Then I drew a line from that and wrote, "stolen jewellery".

The computer finished its start-up sequence and sat waiting for me to use it, but now that I had started scribbling on the pad, I was coming up with more and more bits that I needed to factor in. Someone had killed Jack and though I had no idea what the motive for that might be, it wasn't much of a leap to believe it was linked to stolen jewellery. Last night I thought Jack was joking about the jewel thief thing. I couldn't yet discount that he might have been, but if he hadn't stolen my rings, then where were they? Come to think of it, if he had stolen them, where were they? Had the killer taken them?

I grabbed the mouse and tapped it a few times to bring up the pointer. With no idea what I was doing and nowhere else I needed to be, not that I was allowed to leave anyway, I was going to research as much as I could and see what I could learn. Typing *Jack Langley* into a search bar resulted in a dozen hits for different people. I was able to immediately eliminate half of them because they had photographs that were not the man I knew. The rest I had to click on and then study the information to determine that they too were not the right person. In five minutes, I had no Jack Langleys left.

Had I spelt it wrong? I tried spelling his last name with an extra E - LANGELEY. No hits at all. I bit my lip. Why couldn't I find him and what did that tell me? I picked up the cabin phone and pressed the button to summon Jermaine. He appeared about four seconds later.

'Madam.' I fixed him with a single raised eyebrow. 'How can I help?'

I wanted to restart our conversation about how he should address me, but I didn't have the energy and he looked uncomfortable every time I pushed him to call me by my first name. I chose to let it go.

Looking up at him from my chair by the computer, I said, 'Well, I didn't murder Jack Langley with a knife so what I could really use your help with is clearing my name.' Suddenly, getting Charlie back and working out the issues with our marriage were a secondary concern that felt almost insignificant. Jermaine looked very unsure, like he was good with butler duties, and this fell way, way outside of what he knew how to do. I patted a couch just across from me. 'Take a seat.'

'What can I do to be of assistance, madam?' he asked as he settled into the fabric.

'I have been trying to find out more about the murder victim, but Jack Langley doesn't show up in any search engines I have tried.' I wafted my hand at the computer screen.

'Okay. That should be easy enough, madam. All the passengers have their passport details recorded at central registry when they come on board, so we have a manifest in the event of an emergency.'

'I also need to find the man that was following us today. I don't know how to do that though. Especially now that I am trapped in here and banned from leaving.'

Jermaine pursed his lips. 'Yes, that is a little more difficult. I'm not sure I would be able to identify him again. I couldn't see his face properly with the hat and glasses.'

'No. As a disguise, it served its purpose.' Annoyingly so. If I saw him again, I could confront him and tear his hat and sunglasses off, but how could I send Jermaine to do that? My thoughts were interrupted by a knocking noise. I turned my head toward the door across the other side of the main living area we were in, but that was not where the sound had come from.

'Hello,' said Barbie to get our attention. We swung around to find that she had come in through the kitchen. 'I got no answer at your door,' she said to Jermaine. 'So, I let myself in. I hope that's okay.' The last bit was addressed to me.

'Join us, please,' I replied. 'Are you alright? Was Commander Schooner hard on you?' I wondered if he might have aimed his unpleasantness at her once he was done with me. He displayed no concern in barking orders at her when he disturbed our lunch.

'Oh, I'm fine. He's not nice, but he is like that with everyone.'

'He sure is,' agreed Jermaine.

Barbie was looking at me expectantly. 'Was there something you wanted?' I asked, unsure why she was here.

'Oh. Well, Commander Schooner said I was to arrange some private sessions in the gym.' I groaned internally. 'And he said I had to have a guard with me in case you tried to kill me and escape because you had already killed someone since coming onboard.' She wore a frown on her face that let me know the person she could see did not look like a crazy murderer.

I rolled my eyes. 'Sorry to spoil the fun but I didn't kill anyone.'

'Mrs Fisher is trying to figure out what did happen,' Jermaine interjected. 'We have all kinds of mystery going on here. Missing jewellery, men in disguise ... It's quite exciting,' he said brightly.

79

I rolled my eyes again. 'Exciting isn't the word I would use. I'm accused of murder and under house arrest.'

'Yes, right. Sorry. I got a little carried away, madam' he replied meekly.

Barbie held up her hand. 'So, who is the killer?' she asked.

'That's the bit I have to find out.' Jermaine and Barbie were watching me. I stood up, gathering my thoughts as I paced a little. Their eyes tracked me as I moved around, waiting for me to say something. 'I think we need to first work out why he was killed. The killer could be anyone. There're thousands of crew and passengers on board so …' I had no idea what I was talking about. I was trying to articulate coherent ideas, but I was pulling my concept of how to go about solving this mess from watching daytime detective shows like *Ironside* and *Murder, She Wrote*. 'We have to work out why someone would benefit from his death. Was it revenge? Was it motivated by love or sex?' I was pacing back and forth, a tiny thread of an idea forming as I talked. 'There is a man that we need to find. Jermaine and I have seen him, but we don't know what he looks like because he was wearing a disguise. I can tell you that he is white and probably in his thirties. He fits into this mess somehow and finding him must be my top priority. I need your help though because I can't leave the room.'

I was pacing back and forth as I talked and was facing back toward them when I realised something had been niggling me since Barbie arrived. 'Barbie, how did you get into the suite?'

'I came in through Jermaine's cabin,' she said.

'Which is connected to my kitchen,' I attempted to clarify.

'And isn't being guarded!' Jermaine finished the conclusion I was leading to.

I locked eyes with Barbie, suddenly energised. 'Barbie, I need a makeover.'

She clapped her hands together excitedly, 'Yay!' Then the excited smile was replaced by confusion. 'Why?' she asked.

Sneaking About

Getting out of my suite proved to be easier than I could have possibly imagined because there was a second door that Commander Schooner failed to take into account. Even so, it still opened into the same wide passage as the suite's main door which a pair of burly guards in white uniform were now standing outside.

Barbie and Jermaine disguised me by putting me in a spare uniform from Jermaine's closet. In many ways the outfit choice was brilliant as I had to acknowledge there were so many crew going back and forth that I never paid them any attention.

Why would anyone else?

Buoyed by the hope that I was largely invisible, and coupled with the belief that, unless Commander Schooner had circulated my photograph, almost no one knew me, I was still thoroughly nervous during the twenty-four minutes it took to get from my suite to one of the on-board theatres. The Aurelia, like other cruise ships to my knowledge, put on lots of different shows so Barbie and Jermaine were taking me to one of the backstage dressing rooms.

The anxiety I felt proved to have no foundation as not once did anyone spare a glance in my direction. Although, I will say that lots of eyes tracked Barbie's progress. So many, in fact, and so often, that she didn't even notice it. As you might imagine, the eyes all belonged to scumbag men, some of whom made their ogling so overt that we heard a complaint or, in two cases, a slap on the arm from the men's wives.

It had been my intention to have Barbie dress me up to look far younger, but the uniform worked so well we all agreed I should stick with it.

Barbie said, 'I still think we need to change your hair and face a little.'

'I think there are some wigs in one of the cupboards,' Jermaine added helpfully before ducking out to see what he could find.

Left alone with Barbie, I felt a need to express my thanks. Both were putting their jobs in jeopardy. 'I can't thank you enough for helping me, Barbie.'

'Oh, it's nothing,' she replied.

'It really isn't nothing, Barbie. You could get into hot water if Commander Schooner discovers you smuggled me out.'

Barbie shrugged. She was applying make up to my eyes but stopped to say, 'I had considered that. Fortunately for me, people see a pretty, blonde woman and assume I am stupid. If Commander Schooner quizzes me, I will dazzle him with my dumbest smile and giggle. You would not believe how many men fall for it.'

As she went back to disguising my face, I asked her a question, 'So, what's the deal with you and Jermaine? How did you get to be friends?'

'Oh, Jermaine is just the best,' she grinned. 'We came aboard on the same day just over a year ago, both got lost, and arrived late to Schooner's induction brief. He made us stand up in front of everyone else at the edge of the stage for an hour. I guess we bonded over that. Isn't it just great having a gay BFF though?' she asked.

'I, ah. I don't really know any gay men other than Jermaine. We don't get many overtly homosexual men where I live.'

'Well, it is,' she stated knowingly. 'They don't want anything from you. You don't want anything from them. You can talk about clothes and makeup and boys. It's soooo cool,' she drawled in her California accent.

'He even has the greatest advice about sex. He knows just what to do with a boy's junk, because, you know, he's got one. Once, he told me to …'

Mercifully, Jermaine chose that exact moment to return. He seemed nervous and out of breath, but he was holding a plastic bag that appeared to have a cat in it.

'Ladies,' he said in greeting. Then reaching his hand into the bag and with a flourish and a, 'Ta-dah!' he produced what turned out to not be a cat but was instead a wig.

Of dreadlocks.

'Um,' I started.

'It's the best I could do, madam,' he defended his choice. 'It will hide your hair.'

'Yes, but won't I then look like Bob Marley's white aunt?' I pointed out.

He shrugged. I looked at Barbie for her opinion, but all I got from her was another shrug.

'Okay,' I sighed, 'let's see what it looks like.' Barbie took the hairpiece, came around behind me and slid it on. It certainly covered all my hair. It also made me look ridiculous. 'This won't work,' I said it as I took it off.

Thankfully, both my companions agreed.

'So, what do we do?' asked Jermaine.

I asked, 'How about a hat?'

'Crew don't wear hats,' he replied.

'The chefs do,' Barbie countered.

Then an idea popped into my head. I had to find the mystery man. A man who could be anywhere on board the world's largest ocean liner and might even be wearing a different ridiculous disguise the next time I saw him, so where was the best place to look for him?

At dinner.

He had to eat, so at mealtimes I could be in the restaurants. The crew in the restaurants were the wait staff. There would be no reason for me to be in there unless I was disguised as one of them but then I would look like me. But dressed as a chef, I could hide my hair. It just might work.

'Barbie, do you know any of the chefs well enough to borrow their clothes?'

She thought about that for a moment. 'Brian seems to have a thing for me. I can ask him.'

'Ok then,' I replied, 'Let's find Brian.'

I couldn't say I felt confident now that I was by myself, but I was the one to concoct the stupid plan, and I didn't see how I could back out at this point.

All the restaurants, except for the upper deck, were accessible by all passengers. The upper deck was reserved for the special guests staying in the top two decks of suites. I hadn't known this myself until Jermaine and I started brainstorming where best to hang out and look for the mystery man. Since he was in the upper deck restaurant last night, it stood to reason he must be in one of the best suites and might therefore be reasonably expected to return.

Let's just say I bet all the money on black and didn't have another play if he failed to show. The bit I hadn't counted on was how much I would stand out. I was dressed as a chef, so to the passengers filing in and seeing the wonderful spread of food, I looked like I belonged. However, there were other chefs wearing the same uniform and they were all doing things.

There was a carvery, there was a fresh sushi bar where passengers surrounded the two chefs working there and got to watch the mastery taking place. There was a Chinese kitchen set up in a corner where flames shot up almost continually because the chefs there were adding flare and excitement to what they were doing. I was just milling about near the entrance, hoping I could catch a glimpse of the mystery man when he came in.

If he came in.

Jermaine and Barbie came with me to the door of the restaurant before withdrawing, wishing me luck, and probably praying I would not get caught so they themselves would not be exposed as my accomplices.

Twenty minutes passed as I greeted passengers when they noticed me and tried to look like I belonged.

'What are you doing?' asked a voice from behind me.

I spun around to find another man in chefs' clothing staring down at me. He looked grumpy and a bit sweaty and he had a fat belly that made his apron stick out like it was hiding a fuel tank. His accent was German, but his English came out fluently. I opened my mouth to start lying but he held up his hand to silence me.

'I don't care. Reinhart sent you from the eighteenth deck galley, right? You know we are short staffed, so why it is I find you hiding out here when I need you working? I knew he would send me someone useless.' He grabbed my left arm around the bicep as he turned away, dragging me after him. I could say I resisted but I didn't because he weighed at least twice as much as me and doing so would have caused a scene and drawn unwanted attention.

Ten seconds later I was shoved behind the sushi counter. 'I need Thomas in the kitchen,' the fat chef snarled as he indicated his head to one of the men.

The man quickly finished what he was doing, passed the freshly made green roll thingies to the customer in front of him and darted away.

The fat chef was doing nothing to hide his lack of patience. 'You can make sushi, right?' he asked me. He didn't wait for an answer though, he had other things on his mind.

'I'll take a California roll, please.'

I looked up to find a thin, posh-looking lady with an upper-class English accent staring at me. Around her neck was a string of pearls that looked like they might cost more than a car. I couldn't see her foot, but the way her lips were pursed made me think she was tapping it with impatience.

'Just one moment,' I begged while I went to the sink behind me to wash my hands. I once attended a sushi class with Maggie. It was about three years ago. She booked it because she thought it would be a fun thing to do and it had been, although what I remembered now was that rolling sushi was far harder than it looked.

I could stall no longer so I was going to have to bluff my way through this or abandon the hope of catching the mystery man tonight.

I fixed the lady with a smile. 'California roll, yes?'

'Yes,' she answered a little snippily - I had already wasted enough of her evening.

'What's in that again, please?'

Next to me the young man in the chef's uniform hissed, 'It's a sushi roll, rolled inside-out and containing cucumber, crab meat and avocado.'

Again, I smiled at the lady as I eyed up the ingredients in front of me, trying to find the ones I needed.

'Is this going to take long?' the woman demanded to know.

I lied, 'Not long at all.'

The young man's foot knocked into mine to get my attention. 'I'm making one now. Copy me,' he whispered.

So, I did. His expert hands were a blur though as he laid out rice, neatly sliced avocado and cucumber and delicately added a line of brown crab meat before twisting the bamboo mat like a seasoned professional to produce a six-inch sausage of rice which he then sliced into six perfect rounds.

He handed his over to the gentleman waiting in front of him. I offered mine to the lady, looking up as I did so to a face that looked like I had just shoved a dead pigeon in it.

'What is that?' she asked.

'California roll?' I hazarded.

'After an earthquake,' the man next to her added, chuckling as he departed with his perfect sushi. Mine was less than perfect. So imperfect in fact it was getting the attention of everyone waiting patiently in line for their turn. As we all stared at the plate I held up for the lady, the rice started to fall away from the rolls.

'I think I'll have a salad instead,' she said and walked away.

The young chef leaned in to whisper again, 'I'll make, you serve. Okay?'

I nodded vigorously and that was how it worked. Somehow, I was a sushi sous-chef on board the world's largest ocean liner. I quickly learned that the man's name was Ian. He was from Southampton and said he knew there was no sushi bar in the eighteenth deck restaurant and hadn't expected me to be any good at making it.

We worked like that for half an hour before I looked up to address the next customer in line and found myself face to face with the mystery man. Despite his disguise earlier today and his ridiculous sunglasses last night, I was certain it was him. The hair matched and the shape of his face was the same. My jaw hung open for a second. He was going to recognise me.

'I'll have the Hamachi gunkanmaki, please, with extra wasabi.'

I stared, trying to work out what to say. Was I staring at a murderer? Was he the one who stabbed Jack? How come he hadn't spotted that he was talking to the same woman he was following earlier?

'The Hamachi gunkanmaki, please,' he repeated.

Ian kicked my foot which broke the spell finally. 'Absolutely, sir. That will be just one moment.' He nodded and lost interest in me, peering at his phone. I risked a question. 'Travelling alone, sir?

He lifted his eyes to look at me through his fringe. At least he wasn't wearing the daft hat tonight. Instead, he was dressed much the same as all the other men with a jacket and tie. 'Yes, thank you,' he replied. That he was displeased with the question was clear.

I pressed on anyway because I had just learned something. 'Are you on board for a long trip, or just a short one?' Ian kicked my foot again. This time I ignored him.

Now the mystery man lifted his head to look at me, which made me gulp. Had he just worked out that I was his quarry? He opened his mouth, but all he said was, 'Until I get off.'

If he had identified me, he was doing nothing about it, but with a small lump of terror now forming in my throat, I attempted to deflect his suspicion and asked another question. 'Sorry for the questions, sir. You look like someone famous.' He frowned. 'Are you, sir? Are you someone famous? Can I ask your name?'

'Flint Magnum,' he replied just as Ian handed me the mystery man's sushi. He accepted it with a nod and was gone, forgetting me immediately.

I watched as he wove his way to a table across the air-conditioned lounge. Fumbling to put his phone away, he dropped something. It gave me a perfect reason for speaking to him again as I could now pick it up and hand it back to him. I spotted where he was sitting and acknowledged that it was time to act.

I had to confront him now.

'Excuse me,' the next person in line wanted to be served. I thought about taking their order, but I was only acting the role to spot my mystery man and I couldn't think of a further use for the ruse.

'Sorry, I'm on my break,' I said with a quick smile as I ducked out the back of the sushi shack. Ian called after me, but his voice was lost to the general din of the restaurant as I followed Flint Magnum's path.

He was ahead of me, just thirty feet away and as I closed the distance, I began to compose in my head what I was going to say when I got to him. Reaching the spot where I believed his mystery object fell, I scanned the deck.

My brain insisted it was a bank card – it was that shape - but I couldn't find it. I didn't want to spend too much time looking for it because I was drawing the attention of the passengers around me as I stared at the deck between their tables.

Just as I was about to give up, I spotted it, but as I snagged it from the deck and hurried on, I could tell the item in my hand was paper not plastic. Looking down, I saw the object was a business card. Only a brief glance was needed to show me it wasn't his name displayed.

I went back to searching for the bank card, for I was sure that was what I saw him drop, but after another two minutes of fruitless scrabbling on my hand and knees, I admitted defeat.

I stuffed the business card in my pocket rather than discard it again, since there were passengers watching me, and got back to my feet.

A few paces from his table, I questioned what my approach should be. Did I plonk myself down in the seat opposite him and straight out ask him why he killed Jack Langley? Or should I play it more subtly and let him know that I knew what he did? The only problem with the second option was that I had no idea what anyone had done or why. If he called my bluff, I was stuffed, and if he called to get the attention of the crew, I would quickly find myself in deep water and take my new friends with me.

As it turned out, I didn't get to say or do anything. I was so focussed on my target that I hadn't noticed the white uniform crossing the room to my right. It was on a converging path, emerging from between two tables just a pace ahead of me. The man in the white uniform pulled out the chair I was heading for and sat.

My heart literally stopped, and I got to watch in abject horror as Commander Schooner placed his hat on the table and shook hands with Flint Magnum. He was looking at the man opposite him and ignoring me, the chef's uniform doing as intended and making me invisible. But all he needed to do was look up and he would have me, and I could feel myself about to sneeze. Rather than break my stride and draw attention to myself, I continued onward to pass the table.

As I did so, I got to hear their conversation.

'What will you do now that Mr Langley is dead?' asked Schooner of my mystery man.

I couldn't see his face, it was already behind me, but it was Flint Magnum's voice that replied, 'It is still missing, so my task hasn't changed.'

'Aachooo!' I sneezed.

Commander Schooner turned his head just as I drew level with him.

'Gesundheit.'

I didn't stop moving or speak for fear he might recognise my voice, but he whipped out a meaty hand to grab my arm. I froze in horror. 'Send a waiter over with a gin and tonic. There's a good girl,' he instructed.

I'd been holding my breath so long now I could hear my pulse thumping in my ears, but he let my hand go, smacked me on the rump for good measure, and laughed a dirty laugh as I hurried away having never once taken the time to look at me.

What had I just heard? The man that was holding me captive and accusing me of murder was somehow linked to the man I thought might be the murderer.

And that man was looking for something.

Outside, in the quiet air drifting in off the ocean, I all but collapsed. My poor heart! I thought I was busted, and in the split second between Commander Schooner grabbing my arm and asking for the drink, my brain played out a dozen scenarios that had me mopping decks in the bowels of the ship with a chain between my ankles to them constructing an actual jail cell for me to be held captive in. I sucked in gasps of air as I pulled off my hat and put my head between my knees. My goodness, that was scary. Thankfully, it was a short hop back to my suite and the effort and terror had been worth it as I now had the name of the mystery man.

93

Flint Magnum.

It was an odd name though. It sounded more like a dodgy film star name from the seventies like Rip Torn or Slim Pickens. I was still thinking about the name when I walked up to the security guard outside my suite door.

Oh, my God! I was so lost in my own thoughts I forgot I couldn't just let myself in!

'Can I help you?' the man asked.

I flapped my mouth twice, but no words came out.

'Are you here to take Mrs Fisher's food order?' He didn't recognise me, but then I didn't recognise him and didn't think he had been one of the ones who was searching my suite earlier.

'Ack!' I squeaked, then swallowed and tried again. 'No, sorry, wrong suite.' I turned and hurried away. He had been about to let me in which would have been great, but then might have noticed when the chef failed to ever come back out. To protect my ability to venture out again, I needed to maintain the belief that I was trapped inside.

I kept going in the direction I'd been heading, leaving the security guard behind me. However, Jermaine's door wasn't all that much farther down the passage. Would the guard be watching me and wonder where I was going when I went in through the very next door?

Perhaps it would be better to keep going, find somewhere to lay low and come back later when he was distracted or had changed over for someone else. Deciding it was a good idea, I changed my mind three paces after passing Jermaine's door when I saw the captain coming towards me. He was escorting a nice-looking couple and gesticulating in the same manner he had with me on our way to my suite just a day ago.

I was trapped again. I couldn't see how he could possibly not recognise me if I walked right up to him in this tight passageway. I was in the uniform of a member of his crew. Would he talk to me? Probably.

Panicked, I turned around yet again and went back to Jermaine's door. I grabbed the handle and turned it, desperate to get in before the guard looked my way.

It was locked!

Oh, my Lord!

I wrapped my knuckles on the door as quietly and insistently as I could. The guard was chatting with a pretty, brunette lady, but he was going to look my way soon, and the captain was less than twenty feet behind me.

'Who is it?' came a voice from the other side. It was muffled but it sounded like Jermaine.

'Let me in,' I insisted.

A pause on the other side. 'Who is it, please?'

Sweat ran from my brow as stomach clenching fear caused my voice to squeak, 'It's Patricia,' as quietly as I could.

'Patricia?'

'Mrs Fisher. The resident of the suite. Open the door.'

The door finally opened just before the captain got to me. My weight was against it so I tumbled inside, bowling Jermaine to the deck as I went head over heels to land on the carpet in a heap.

From my inverted position I looked up to discover that it was not, in fact, Jermaine, but an altogether different person I was looking at. Confused, I looked around as I tried to right myself. This wasn't even Jermaine's room.

I had just busted my way into the wrong butler's cabin!

Evening

Having apologised and excused myself, I left the poor man alone and found myself back in the sunlit passage once more. Somehow, in finding myself trapped between the captain and the security guard, in my panic I missed that there was a second door next to Jermaine's. The suite next to mine must be a reverse image which put the butler's accommodation right on the other side of the wall from Jermaine's.

This time, when I knocked on the right door, it was Jermaine's face I saw when it opened. Filled with relief, I wrapped him in a hug the moment he shut the world outside. Sensing his discomfort, I pushed away after only a second or so.

'Sorry. That was more ... adventurous than I expected. I ran into Commander Schooner, but he didn't recognise me.'

Jermaine blew out his breath in horror. 'What happened, madam?'

'I'll tell you about it in a minute. I need to get out of this outfit.' The chef clothes had done the trick, but they didn't really fit me. The waist band was cutting my belly in two which was mostly about the size of my belly rather than the waist of the trousers, which reminded me I was supposed to be getting more exercise with Barbie.

A vague hope that she might have forgotten surfaced.

'Hi, Patty,' she called out brightly as she came through Jermaine's door. 'Are you ready for your next session?'

Nuts!

'We need to get this one in now so you have enough time to rest and recover before bed.' I wanted to ask if she was joking but I already knew that she wasn't. 'You'll get sore if we don't keep the muscles supple

97

though, so we need to start with a massage.' That sounded more like it. 'I can do that here or at the gym, whichever you prefer.'

'I'll get changed then,' I tried to keep the sigh from my voice as I accepted my fate. Barbie and Jermaine followed me through from his adjoining quarters firing questions as they came.

'How did it go?' Barbie wanted to know.

'Did you find the mystery man, madam?' Jermaine asked.

Somehow, I'd forgotten to mention the biggest news of the evening.

Halfway through undoing my chef's tunic, I stopped and turned back to face my two ... mentally I stopped to consider how it was that I framed my relationship with Jermaine and Barbie. They weren't exactly friends, not yet anyway since I had only met them yesterday, but I wasn't sure what else to call them. Accomplices made it sound like I was guilty of something, which I wasn't so I labelled them as teammates - they were on Team Patricia.

Anyway, their questions warranted answers, so I told them about finding myself making sushi and how the mystery man suddenly appeared in front of me.

'Flint Magnum,' Jermaine repeated the name, wrinkling his nose as if a bad smell had just invaded it. 'That doesn't sound real.'

'I know, right?' I couldn't agree more. 'He sounds like he should work in the adult film industry or something.'

'So, what now?' asked Barbie.

'You mentioned a central registry of all passengers earlier,' I reminded Jermaine. 'Can you find his name on that and find out what room he is in?

Then maybe we can follow him and see what he is up to.' I chose not to add that I needed to break into his room and search it for clues. I was certain that would not be well received and would absolutely change Barbie and Jermaine from teammates into accomplices.

Jermaine nodded. 'I shall attend to that now, madam.' He indicated back toward my kitchen and the door to his adjoining cabin. 'I should have the information before you return from the gym.' He saw my expression and flicked his eyes to Barbie and then back to me. 'You are going to the gym?' he sought to confirm.

'We are,' said Barbie, jumping to her feet. Seeing me not moving, she asked, 'We are, aren't we?' I didn't really want to but the only place I was allowed to visit was the gym so even though I had been out for the last hour, I felt that I should take the chance I was given and suffer through another round of sweaty, breathless exercise with the blonde goddess now waiting for my answer. She did say she was going to give me a massage. Reluctantly I nodded my head.

'Yay!' She clapped her hands in excitement.

'I'll get changed then. Oh, hold on,' a ray of hope shone on me. 'I'm not sure I have any clean gym clothes to wear.'

'I laundered and pressed your clothes from earlier already, madam' revealed Jermaine, super helpfully.

I muttered under my breath and stomped off to find my clean gym clothes. 'I'll need to buy some new ones. Is there a shop here that sells such things?' I called back from the bedroom.

Barbie's voice echoed through from the living area, 'Sure, Patty. You can buy everything on board.'

'Can you see if the security guy will let us go there and whether he is the one escorting me to the gym or if he needs to call for someone else, please?'

Barbie called through again to let me know she was on her way to the door. I heard a brief exchange, the tinkling sound of her laugh as the security guy was no doubt trying to entertain his way into her knickers, and the sound of the door closing again.

With my baggy, shapeless shorts, and t-shirt on over a big pair of knickers and a sports bra, I stared at the mirror. Next to Barbie I looked ridiculous. To be fair, so would more than ninety-nine percent of women on the planet but they didn't have to stand next to her. Through my t-shirt, I could see the roll of belly fat resting on the top of my shorts. I added a sweatshirt to cover it up. It wasn't much better, but it helped, even if it did mean I would sweat like a pig.

I stepped out of my bedroom to find the security guy in my living room. 'Aren't you supposed to wait outside?' I accused him.

He was six feet and a couple of inches of ramrod straight military-looking rigidness. His hair was cut short to the back and sides and set neatly on top with a side parting. He wore his uniform as if he were about to go on parade and beneath it his muscular frame stretched the fabric over his biceps, shoulders, chest … you get the picture.

He held up a hand which I believed was meant to instruct me to stop moving. It didn't work, I just kept moving and he had to track across the room to block my route to the door.

'Madam, if you plan to leave the suite, I am under instruction to search you for weapons.'

That stopped me.

I gawped at him. 'You have got to be kidding.' He didn't bother to reply. 'I'm a fifty-two-year-old, overweight woman from the leafy suburbs of rural England. Just what is it you think I might have stashed in my knickers? A Kalashnikov? A few grenades?' I was staring at him to see if his impassive face had any other expressions in its repertoire. Not so far. 'I could tell you that I didn't kill Jack Langley but since no one seems to want to believe that one, please search away.' He didn't move, perhaps unsure what he was supposed to do. 'Tell me. Will you be looking in my body cavities as well?'

That made his featureless face twitch. Involuntarily, a grimace tugged at his mouth. Teasing hadn't been as much fun as I thought though. Bored, I lifted my sweatshirt to show the thin t-shirt beneath it and turned about. 'See? No guns, knives or nunchucks.'

All I got was a nod. We were ready to go. Then he put his hand to his ear where a small curly wire ran to an earpiece. He nodded to an unseen person only he could hear and spoke into the cuff of his uniform. Then he looked at me. 'Commander Schooner is on his way, madam. Please wait here.'

I flapped my arms in frustration. I didn't exactly want to go to the gym, but I certainly didn't want to be told I couldn't go. As my frustration rose, dragging my anger with it, I forced myself to stay calm. Two slow breaths later, I reversed into a chaise-lounge, and offered the guard a smile. Moments later he turned and opened the door to allow an angry looking Commander Schooner in.

He wasted no time on pleasantries and got straight on with being himself.

'How did you do it?'

My mouth opened as an impulse reaction, but I closed it again without answering his question. How could I possibly answer him? How had I done what?

'Hmmm?' he tried again, clearly expecting me to say something.

It was Barbie who broke the stand-off. 'What has happened, sir?'

Commander Schooner, still squinting at me with his narrow, accusing eyes, cast his gaze at Barbie for a second before bringing it back to me again. 'Someone mutilated Jack Langley's body. One of Mrs Fisher's accomplices, no doubt.'

'Ewwww,' said Barbie while pulling a convincingly disgusted face.

I gave him a bored look. 'Why would I want to do anything to Jack Langley's body?'

His upper lip twitched in annoyance. 'I intend to find out.' Then he spun on his heel and left again, leaving me with a fresh mystery to ponder.

Someone chose to mutilate Jack Langley's dead body. What on earth would they have done that for? I thought about it for a moment, but no plausible reason presented itself.

'Shall we go?' asked Barbie, her smile back in place. Had she already forgotten the body mutilation?

Almost two hours later, I stumbled back through the door and fell onto the couch. Okay, the two hours started with a twenty-minute massage and ended with a twenty-minute warm down, but I was still dying.

'Everything all right, madam?' asked Jermaine, appearing from the kitchen. He was still dressed in his immaculate butler outfit.

'Don't you ever take that off?' I asked from my prone position.

'Of course, madam,' he replied. 'At bedtime.'

'Did you find Flint Magnum?'

Jermaine crossed the room to stand near the high-backed chairs opposite the couch. 'No record of him, I'm afraid, madam. He gave you a made-up name.'

The sneaky little toad.

So, what now, Patricia? my brain wanted to know. I didn't have an answer. I was getting tired. The hangover from last night was long forgotten, any ill effects well out of my system, but the fatigue caused by a poor night's sleep had caught up with me. Undoubtedly it was exacerbated by the additional exercise and the workout my adrenal system had received today combined with consuming a fraction of the calories I would usually ingest.

If I closed my eyes right now, I would be asleep in seconds, but I was just as hungry as I was tired, and Barbie was bringing me dinner. Leaving the gym, she promised to select me something that would tantalise my taste buds and satisfy my cravings as well as fill me up and replenish my energy reserves. I really hoped what she had in mind was a steak and three gin and tonics, but I expected to be disappointed.

In the end, it was morning when I found out what she had for me because despite my intentions, I fell asleep on the wide, soft couch and woke up several hours later with a blanket over me and a note from Jermaine requesting that I call him upon waking so he could settle me correctly. I wasn't sure what that meant, but I had been putting myself to bed for more than forty years and could manage it one more time at least.

Madeira

The ship docked in Madeira at some point in the night. When I woke, it took me a while to work out that the difference I could perceive was the missing distant hum of the ship churning through the water.

From my private sun terrace, the view was green hills rising into the distance and wide sandy beaches to my left and right beyond the port. Of course, with a ship this size, the ports it went to had to be substantial and this one lay at the foot of a city, its buildings stretching inland and away into the hills.

'What city is that?' I asked Jermaine as he poured coffee from a silver coffee pot into my delicate porcelain cup.

'Funchal, madam.' I squinted at him. I guess he knew I was going to complain about the madam thing again because he headed me off before I could speak.

'Madam, if it pleases you, I had to work hard to attain this position. My duties as butler to the Royal Suite come with a certain amount of ceremony and as such, I feel uncomfortable addressing you informally. I feel it … undermines the role.' He delivered what I believed was a long-considered message without the slightest gesticulation.

'Okay, Jermaine.' I couldn't present an argument, so I was going to be madam whenever he spoke to me. It wasn't something I hated; it just didn't seem to fit.

'Is there a pair of binoculars in the room?' I asked. 'Since I am not permitted to go ashore, I would like to look a little closer than I can with just my eyes.'

'Very good, madam.' Jermaine butlered away to return just a few moments later with a large case shaped roughly the same as a large pair of binoculars.

Thanking him, I took them from his hands once he extracted them from the case and made sure they were clean, then I trained them on the crowds of people leaving the ship. I had no interest in the island ahead of me. Or rather, I did, but since I wasn't going to get to explore it, I figured I might as well tell myself I didn't and do something constructive instead.

The question I had, was whether I would be able to spot Flint Magnum from up here or not. The binoculars were certainly powerful enough. So powerful, in fact, that when I zoomed in, I could tell if men needed to clip the hair in their ears. I had to pan back to a wider view just to make out faces.

Jermaine took up a rigidly upright position next to me. He was determined to treat me like royalty.

Without taking my eyes off the crowd making their way inland, I said, 'You know, I clean toilets in rich people's homes for a living.'

He nodded stiffly. 'Nevertheless, you are the lady of this ship and I intend to see you treated as one.'

'That's good of you, Jermaine. However, I'm not exactly the lady of the ship while I am locked away in here.' He had no response to give, nor did I expect one. My circumstances were not his fault. I had another question for him though, 'Can I ask where you are from?'

'Jamaica, madam.'

'Really? How is it then that you sound like you grew up in Chelsea?' I took the binoculars away from my face to see how he reacted to my prying. He looked embarrassed.

'I, um. I didn't think the Jamaican accent went with the role, madam,' he supplied, hanging his head guiltily.

I had to laugh. 'So your accent is completely fake? Where did you learn it?'

He looked up to meet my eyes. 'Watching Downton Abbey.'

I laughed again.

'Good morning, guys,' said Barbie in her usual relaxed, breezy manner as she joined us in the sunshine. To the side of me, as I watched through my binoculars, the two of them chatted about something. I continued to scan the crowd.

Then, I spotted something for a half second that I then couldn't find again - I swear I saw Flint Magnum. I jumped up for a better look as if moving forward two feet would make a difference. I spotted him again though, one hundred yards from the boat and funnelling along with everyone else.

He was wearing knee-length, bright orange surfer shorts with writing down the side and a light blue vest top that showed off his milky skin. He had a terrible part-tan where his forearms had caught the sun but stopped halfway up his biceps. His calves were so white they were almost translucent. That he might go ashore was nothing more than a lucky guess, but there he was, and I knew what he was wearing.

'I'm going ashore,' I announced. Barbie and Jermaine just stared at me. 'The chef disguise won't work this time. I need something better.'

107

'Um,' said Barbie, 'I have an idea, but you might not like it.'

'Why, what is it?' I asked.

'No. Not *you* might not like it,' she replied, turning to face Jermaine. 'You might not like it.'

Ten minutes later when she returned, I understood why. I was going to leave the ship pretending to be a Jamaican.

'This is culturally insensitive,' Jermaine insisted several times while he helped Barbie cover my face, arms, and any other exposed skin in thick dark brown makeup she got from a friend who worked in the ship's entertainment department. Add sunglasses, the dreadlock wig, a few bits of jewellery, and a brightly coloured skirt, and from a distance, if a person were blind, then maybe I would pass muster.

I didn't look like Patricia Fisher though and that was the point. Though I felt uncomfortable about it, I was going to pose as Jermaine's mother and Barbie was coming as his pretend girlfriend.

Many decks down, we joined the throng of passengers filing slowly out of the ship and onto the dock that led into Funchal. I could have avoided the queue and left via the royal suites' private entrance/exit. However, that would have exposed me to the captain who I could see once again greeting and well-wishing the top paying passengers as they left the ship. They were being collected in golf carts which then drove around the riffraff of normal people to get to Funchal proper without their delicate feet having to exercise.

None of the crew paid me any attention, nor did I expect them to. This was a holiday cruise ship, and the crew were not looking out for a suspected killer fleeing from justice. I doubted many even knew about me or Jack Langley. Once again, I was invisible but unlike yesterday evening in the restaurant when I had been expecting someone to reveal who I was at any second, today I felt relaxed and almost happy.

Jermaine, on the other hand, looked terrified and that was my fault. Even though he believed I was innocent, it would cost him his job if we got caught. Smuggling me off the ship was an enormous risk, and he knew it.

Barbie, in contrast, was acting as if this was just a lovely day out. Her biggest concern was over my insistence we had no time for a morning work-out. My assurances that we could go harder at it later - after we had caught and exposed Flint Magnum as the real killer - was only just enough to convince her.

Of course, now we were off the ship and heading into Funchal, I had to admit that I had no idea how to find our quarry. He left the ship more than half an hour before us and could be in the vast city of Funchal by now. He could be in a bar, or heading to the beach, or even going to a brothel where he planned to spend the whole day for all I knew.

Jermaine asked how I planned to find him.

My answer - the use of blind luck. It was all I had and since I was desperate, I saw no choice but to go with it.

Jermaine and Barbie held hands and looked like a genuine couple. Jermaine was wearing normal person clothes for the first time since I met him, which for him meant a skin-tight top in Day-Glo pink and pair of short denim hot pants that Daisy Duke might have blushed at. He looked ready to party with Mardi Gras bead necklaces around his neck and left wrist. On his feet he wore strappy sandals. I had a pair just like them, but his were twice the size because his feet were huge.

Beside him, Barbie was showing just how perfect her body was in a tiny red bikini that barely covered the crack of her backside. Wrapped around her was a lace sarong that did nothing to cover her up and here's the thing about Barbie – she looks like a Barbie doll. You remember the ridiculous, gravity defying boobs and impossibly small waist that Barbie dolls all sport? Well they could have used Miss Berkeley as a model. Oh, to be twenty-two again.

In their summer outfits, they were doing fine in the heat. As part of my disguise I had gone with a shawl to cover as much of my exposed brown skin as possible and I was already starting to sweat. Would the makeup run off? It made my face itch terribly - the temptation to scratch myself was almost overwhelming though I knew I would most certainly ruin the disguise the second I did so.

At the end of the jetty, we began to meet men hawking their wares - street sellers with all manner of worthless rubbish they were pushing on the tourists pouring from the ship. I pushed through them with Jermaine and Barbie just ahead of me, my eyes constantly vigilant for Jack's killer.

He was nowhere to be seen.

We spent the first hour going in and out of all the bars and eateries close to the port. There were a few tourists in them that might have been from the ship, but food and drink were plentiful on board, so why would someone come ashore and go directly into a bar?

'What else might he get up to?' Jermaine asked. None of us had an answer though because there were too many options. He might be culturally inclined and have jumped on a bus to get to a museum or he might be a sex tourist and genuinely be in a brothel.

Splitting up to look for him separately was discussed and dismissed, we were better off together and no one wanted to find themselves alone with the killer.

The heat and the lack of progress led us to a bar not far from the port. It was dark inside, and gaudily decorated with occult symbols and strange paraphernalia. Behind the bar were skulls – fake, I hoped – stuffed crows, and a crystal ball.

When I asked why Jermaine chose this place above all the nicer looking ones around us, he claimed they made a good Espetada. I had no idea what one of them was, but discovered it was a skewer of barbecued garlic pork served with a circular flat bread called bolo de caco. It came with a side of rice and a basic salad, and would have been a nice lunch if Barbie hadn't insisted I order my salad without dressing and banned me from eating the bread. She also told Jermaine he needed to cut back on his carbs, but he stuck his tongue out at her, making her laugh and somehow getting him off the hook.

We drank water, not that Barbie would have let me have the cool, refreshing beer I could see being poured at the bar, but in deference to the midday heat it was undoubtedly the right thing to keep us hydrated.

The ship was due to sail at seven o'clock. The passengers were requested back on board by six, so at just after noon, when the waiter in the little bar we were in collected our plates, there was a lot of day left to kill. Not only was I getting bored, but my butt was getting sore from the cheap plastic seat on which I was perched.

'What do we do if we don't find him, madam?' asked Jermaine.

It was a good question, and one I had been working on for the past half an hour.

'If we assume we have not missed him,' I started, 'then he must pass us to get back on board at some point, right?' Jermaine nodded in reply, but Barbie's focus was on something across the street.

'Isn't that him there?' she asked, pointing across the street from the café place we were sitting in. 'Milk bottle legs with board shorts and a vest?'

Jermaine swiped her arm downwards as the man turned around but sure enough. There he was.

All right then. Action time.

I stood up. 'What are you going to do?' asked Barbie, also beginning to get out of her chair.

'I don't know. Probably straight out ask him why he killed Jack. Or maybe wrestle him to the ground and grab his passport so I can find out his real name.' I should have been terrified at the prospect of confronting the man, but I was significantly more angry than I was scared. For now, for whatever reason, mousey Patricia had taken a vacation and a new version of me was behind the wheel.

As I stepped out from under the awning at the front of the café, Jermaine grabbed my hand, 'Wait, madam. I have a better idea.'

I paused, glancing at Flint Magnum to check if he had seen me. I was forgetting, of course, that if he had, there was little chance he would recognise the woman beneath the makeup. However, he was looking at a stand of sunglasses outside a shop across the street.

'What's your idea?' I asked my butler.

Jermaine let go my hand but turned his attention to his blonde friend.

'Barbie, can you keep him busy for a few minutes?'

She raised her eyebrows. 'What should I do?'

Jermaine cocked a hip and shot her a look. 'Seriously? Girlfriend, you are the finest woman on the face of the Earth. All you need to do is stand in the street and he won't see anything else happening around him. Go and talk to him.'

She glanced at Flint Magnum in his terrible shorts and vest.

'What if he doesn't like me? What if he is gay?'

Jermaine chuckled, 'He's not gay.'

'How can you tell?' she asked.

'I can tell.'

While their exchange was going on, I was getting impatient. 'What's the plan?'

Jermaine shooed Barbie across the road with a final instruction, 'Bring him to the fortune teller at the back of the bar in ten minutes.' Then he turned to me. 'Do you think you can pretend to be a medium, madam?'

'A medium?'

Jermaine grabbed my hand, tugging me behind him as he headed for the bar.

'Yes, a medium, madam. You know? Like a fortune teller?' He waved his hand at the barman to get his attention. 'My aunt was a fortune teller. Made the whole thing up her entire career. Said it was the easiest job going because fools would believe anything. All you had to do was pick up on little cues.' He pointed to my left hand. 'Like a recently absent ring. She

113

might say that she could sense a broken heart or some rubbish like that. Soon they would be telling her all kinds of stuff about themselves so that she could pick that apart and waste fifteen minutes of their time while giving them nothing but an act.' The barman arrived. 'Can we borrow that, sir?' Jermaine asked, pointing to a shelf behind the bar.

'This?' the barman confirmed, then lifted the object Jermaine wanted off the shelf. He held it back before handing it over though. 'You're not going to do anything weird with it are you?'

'No, sir,' Jermaine assured him. 'We are just going to sit in the back corner of the bar and see if we are attuned to the mystic powers today.' The barman cocked an eyebrow but handed the crystal ball over anyway.

'So, do you think you can do the medium thing, madam?' Jermaine asked.

'I guess, but why?' Mostly I wasn't thinking why. I was thinking I was more of a large than a medium. I kept that thought to myself though.

'If you confront him as Patricia Fisher and ask him if he murdered Jack Langley, he will probably say no and what do you do then? If instead you play the part of the fortune teller and pretend you know things about him because the spirits are talking to you, then you can reveal that you believe he travels under a false identity and that he has dealings with a dead man. You get where I am going with this? I'll set my phone to record it ...'

'And I have to trick him into admitting to the murder.' It was a simple plan, but brilliant, nevertheless. It was certainly superior to my daft plan of poke him in the chest until he gave in and confessed.

From our position at the back of the bar, I could still see across the street. Barbie was chatting with the man I knew as Flint Magnum and being tactile - touching his arm, laughing at something he said - and it was clear he was going to do anything the Baywatch babe in the bikini asked. It was no surprise when she looped her arm through his and led him toward the bar.

'Ooh, here they come. Quick, get in position, madam,' squealed Jermaine excitedly. He placed the crystal ball on the table. We were in the back corner of the mostly empty bar. I placed my glass of water on the table and settled into one of the chairs as Jermaine put his phone under the black tablecloth. It couldn't be seen but would hopefully still record what was being said.

I could see that Barbie was playing her part convincingly. Of course, blonde bimbo was an easy role to play if, like she said yesterday, people expected her to be dumb just because she is blonde and pretty.

She led Flint to the bar across the room from us without looking our way. She laughed about something and had Flint buy her a drink. His arm was looped around her waist already, his hand resting on her left hip and unwilling to let go as if he might not be able to get it back there again.

Jermaine set off. 'I'm going to get them, madam.' He walked to the bar, his accent now hard Jamaican instead of his clipped butler's English. 'Fortunes read, mon,' he announced as he approached them. They were the only people at the bar so he couldn't be talking to anyone else.

'No thanks,' replied Flint without even bothering to turn his head.

'Accurate predictions, mon. Don't miss out. Find out now if this lady is in your future.' Jermaine's hard sell didn't seem be having any effect on Flint until Barbie spoke.

'Ooh, yes, let's see what the fortune teller has to say about tonight,' she purred at him while leaning in close enough that her boobs squashed against his chest.

Suddenly, getting his fortune read was a cracking idea.

'Come along, come along,' I beckoned, trying to copy Jermaine's Jamaican accent. I should have practised it earlier because now I was giving it a go, I thought I sounded utterly fake. Changing it now would be even worse, so we were stuck with it. 'Fortunes read, predictions given.'

'How much?' asked Flint as he sat himself in the seat opposite me. Jermaine deftly swung a second seat in for Barbie to sit beside him.

The question caught me out. What did a fortune teller charge?

'Ten dollars US,' supplied Jermaine, saving me.

Flint shrugged in acknowledgement but didn't reach for his wallet. 'Tell me my future then,' he encouraged, derision dripping from his voice. 'Impress me.'

I was trying to not panic as I raised my hands and wafted them ridiculously around the crystal ball. I had not been given enough time to think about what I wanted to say or how I needed to act so now I was waving my arms around and trying to form a coherent sentence in my head.

'The spirits are circling,' I said, my eyes closed. 'They are whispering to me.'

'Yeah?' he all but laughed. 'What are they saying?'

I snapped my eyes open and fixed him with a stare. 'They say you have a terrible secret.' I was feeling my way into the role now. 'They say you are not who you tell people you are.'

His wide eyes were looking back at me; just like that I'd managed to throw him off balance. It made me feel powerful. Now I needed to milk it.

'The spirits are telling me you call yourself ...' I dragged the sentence out for effect before finishing with, '... Flint Magnum.'

He looked shocked. How could the strange lady sitting across from him know his name?

'What is your real name?' I asked.

Under my spell, he didn't resist at all. 'Neil Hammond.' The name came out at a volume just above a whisper.

I had his name! Now it was time to press him for more. I closed my eyes again and did some more of the arm waving thing since he was buying my nonsense.

'The spirits tell me you are alone. You are on a voyage. Spirits, why is he on this voyage?' I asked the air. I opened my eyes again. 'Are you on this voyage for a purpose?'

Slowly he nodded.

'You are working, not taking a holiday. You are following someone. The spirits say you are frustrated.'

'Yeah,' he agreed, 'really frustrated.'

I let my eyes roll back in a fake display of communing with the other side. 'The spirits are angry. They tell me you carry a great burden.'

'Great burden?' he echoed.

'They know what you did. They are whispering to me.'

'What did I do?'

I began to increase the volume of my voice, 'They say you did something terrible!' Louder yet. 'They say you took a man's life!' I brought

117

my eyes down to stare at his again. 'The spirits need you to say the name of the man!' Finally, I reached a crescendo - I was all but shouting at him, 'Say the name of the man you murdered!'

'Murdered?' Instead of the wide look of incredulity he'd shown a minute ago when he was surprised by the way I knew facts about him, now he just looked confused. 'Why would the spirits think I killed someone?'

'Say the name of the man you murdered!' I repeated, praying he would drop the act and confess for the recording.

The man formerly known as Flint Magnum sat back in his chair and slowly folded his arms. He was staring at me, sizing me up or something. He tilted his head to the side as if trying to look at me from a different angle. Then he looked at Jermaine and finally swung his attention to Barbie. He nodded to himself, reaching a conclusion, then leapt from his chair, diving across the table and lunging for my face.

I screamed in surprise but couldn't stop the crazed killer before he got to me. The spike of adrenaline sent my pulse through the roof as I tried to recoil away from his hands. Was he going to throttle me?

Jermaine sprang forward to come to my help, but he wasn't needed. Flint Magnum, for that was what my brain continued to label him, sat back down in his chair triumphantly holding my dreadlock wig.

'That's a good disguise,' he said. Then his eyes flared again as he took in my blonde hair and finally recognised me. As his eyes went wide as saucers, he leaped backward from his chair, getting distance between him and the three of us. He pointed a shaking hand, 'You're the crazy chick that killed Jack Langley with a knife! Stabbed him in the back after he seduced you in the bar.'

'I killed him?' I repeated incredulously. 'I killed him?'

'You see?' he announced as if he had an audience. 'She admits it.'

'I didn't kill Jack. You did!'

'Me? Why would I kill him?' Flint Magnum questioned. 'I was still trying to prove he took it.'

There was a pregnant pause while we all stared at each other.

It was Jermaine that broke the spell. 'Hold on. Are you saying that you didn't kill Jack Langley?'

Flint Magnum, Neil Hammond, or whatever the heck his name was, swivelled his head to stare at Jermaine, then scanned around to take in both me and Barbie. He sighed and let his shoulders droop.

'I was employed by … a certain lady of high breeding whose husband was somewhat neglectful of her needs. She found solace with a man who I believe to be Jack Langley while on the Aurelia but then discovered her fifteen carat diamond earrings and matching necklace were missing along with a stack of other jewels. I am supposed to recover them. I thought I had the right man, and it took a few days to learn his patterns.' He arrowed accusing eyes at me. 'Just when I was going to strike, you swooped in and distracted him. I couldn't get near him because you were playing the part of the drunk.' I blushed beneath the makeup. 'I gave up when I saw him go into your suite with you.'

'It wasn't what it seemed,' I protested, but Flint Magnum had no interest in what I had to say.

'Next morning, he was dead, and until now I assumed you killed him. Right now, though, with this vaudeville act, I have to question whether you are capable.' He fixed me with a stare. 'Tell me, what were you doing in his cabin yesterday morning?'

I met his stare, 'He took my wedding rings. And my purse. I only came on board two days ago. I had no idea who he was and certainly have no idea what he had been up to.'

'So, you didn't kill him?' Flint asked, his tone utterly serious.

'No!' I squeaked, exasperated at the concept. 'But I am trying to work out who did and why so that I can clear my name.'

He came back toward me and sat back in the chair next to Barbie. He turned to her.

'I was fooled, you know. I shouldn't have been, pretty girl like you. I should have known your interest in me couldn't be genuine.' Then he turned his gaze back to me. 'Jack was probably responsible for stealing jewellery from a lot of different women. Someone has been preying on rich widows and the like for months, but they had no idea who it was until I was hired. Commander Schooner was only too happy to have me on board. I was going to solve the crime for him. All I needed was to catch Jack Langley in the act. That would give us cause to search his cabin.' That explained why Commander Schooner was at his table last night. 'Jack Langley ...' Flint had been about to say something but stopped himself. Before I could prompt him, he changed tack. 'None of the jewellery was found in his cabin. As I understand it, it wasn't in yours either. What did you do with it?'

Jermaine stepped in. 'Don't you understand? Mrs Fisher had nothing to do with any of this. She is totally innocent.'

'Mrs Fisher?' Flint frowned in confusion, then the light of realisation hit. 'You're her butler. Aren't you? I thought I recognised you.'

120

'Yes, you were tailing us yesterday after we saw you hiding in a flowerpot outside Jack's room,' I butted in.

'You spotted me?' Flint asked. He sounded confused by the concept.

'What? You think you are a master of disguise or something?'

He jerked forward in his chair, getting his face closer to mine. 'I *am* a master of disguise,' his voice was indignant and defensive. I wanted to point out that he was rubbish at disguise, but I refrained. Now was not the time.

Everything was topsy-turvy.

I snuck off the ship scared but exhilarated because I thought I was going to expose a killer. Instead, I had a man who was ... what? Some kind of detective for hire? None of it mattered. I had pinned all my hopes on exposing this man as the killer. How did I clear my name now?

Hanging my head in bewilderment, I said, 'I need a gin.'

'No, Patty!' snapped Barbie. 'Sparkling water. That's what you want. Stay hydrated.' She gave me a big supportive grin.

'Oh, God,' I groaned.

Jermaine moved in next to me, his hand coming to rest on my shoulder supportively. 'How may I assist you, madam?'

I tilted my head up to look at him. 'I just realised I have to smuggle my way back onto the damned ship.'

'Oh, yeah,' drawled Flint Magnum with a smug smile. 'You're supposed to be under house arrest.'

'Yes. Thank you for reminding me. Can I have my wig back now?'

'Oh. Oh, yeah, sure.' He handed it over and Jermaine helped me to get it in place. 'You really don't have the jewellery, do you?'

I stared up to heaven wondering what I was going to have to do to get people to believe me.

Sensing my infuriation, he said, 'I'm going to take that as a no.' He stood up to leave. 'So, where is it then?' he muttered under his breath. 'I gotta find out who took it. Man, I thought I was getting close.' Shaking his head, he was starting to walk away when I called him back.

'Do you want to team up?'

'Huh?'

'Do you want to team up?' He was staring at me with his mouth open. 'Look. The way I see it, whoever killed Jack, probably took the jewellery. You and I are looking for the same person.'

'I suppose we are,' he chewed his lip a bit, 'I'll think about it.'

My jaw dropped. 'You'll think about it?' I shrieked. 'You'll think about it? They plan to throw me into a jail cell in St Kitts. You know I'm not guilty and that we both want the same thing, and you'll think about it?'

'Not my problem, toots. I didn't get you into this. Besides, I don't know that you are innocent, I only know that it is the story you are sticking to. I'm just here to find the missing jewellery and get paid.' He kept going, heading for the exit. 'Good luck with the fortune teller business.'

I'd had enough. 'Let's get back to the ship, shall we? I can't take much more time in this heat with all this awful makeup on.'

The walk back to the ship took less than ten minutes and there was almost no queue to get back on because it was still several hours before

122

we were due to sail. There was a team of ship's security checking passports though as the passengers returning to the ship filed on board. I was going to have to show them mine.

'Jermaine,' I hissed as we approached the ship. 'What do we do?'

The short line of people was moving forward; there was hardly any time at all to come up with a plan. Jermaine gripped my hand, but he looked nervous too. His job was on the line for helping me if we got caught.

The problem with showing my passport was that I didn't have one. Urgently, I whispered questions at Jermaine, 'Will they let me on board without a passport? You know they will see that I am wearing makeup to disguise myself the second they take a proper look at me.'

'Oh boy. This is a problem, madam,' Jermaine muttered. He was trying to not move forward as people joined the queue behind us. His eyes were wide and filled with panic as he looked about for a miracle.

Barbie saw us whispering and leaned in. 'What's up, guys?' Jermaine explained about the problem with my passport.

'What if we go and get all the makeup off?' she asked.

'I don't think that many makeup wipes exist, and it doesn't deal with the fact that I have no passport. Plus, without my disguise, if we do somehow get back on board I then have to get through the ship and back into my suite without anyone recognising me.' I could feel my own panic rising.

We were next in line. It was seconds until I was discovered. Why hadn't I thought about getting back on the boat?

Jermaine bent his head slightly and whispered from the side of his mouth, 'Faint, madam.'

'What?'

'Faint. Swoon.' When I looked at him to check I understood, he hissed, 'Quickly, madam.'

Theatrically, I lifted a hand to my forehead, spun and folded into a ragged heap on the ground. Jermaine just about got his arms under me and called for Barbie to help. My eyes were closed, of course, but I could hear Jermaine demanding the security pair checking passports and welcoming passengers back on board come to my aid.

'She's had a bit much to drink. Here's my ID. I'm the butler for the Windsor Suite and this is the guest staying there. We need to get her back on board and up to her suite now.'

'I need to check her passport,' a polite but insistent male voice said.

'I'll bring it back down in a minute,' Jermaine promised.

'But ...'

Jermaine cut him off, 'What is it the captain says about the guests in the royal suites?'

The same voice sighed. 'We give them whatever they ask for and everything they need.' I could hear that it didn't sit well with the man, but he was going to let Jermaine take me aboard anyway.

The sunlight hitting my eyelids was suddenly gone as I was carried onto the ship. The sound changed as we went inside, the enclosed space reflecting an echoing tinny noise. There were voices coming from other passengers around us and I had to keep up the pretence until Team Patricia decided it was safe to do otherwise.

'You can put your feet down, madam,' Jermaine whispered in my ear.

I opened my eyes and looked around. 'Where are we?'

'Girls' restroom,' said Barbie.

I breathed a sigh of relief. 'Well done, guys. I thought I was busted then for sure.'

'We all would have been,' said Jermaine. 'Let's get back to your suite where we can relax and think about our next move.'

'This undercover stuff is so exciting,' giggled Barbie.

'Exciting, yes,' said Jermaine as we reached a bank of elevators. It was clear he didn't think exciting was the right word. 'Just the guard outside your suite to get by and we will be safe.'

The guard wasn't there though. We took the long route so that we came to Jermaine's door first and didn't have to walk in front of the guard to get there, but it was clear long before we reached Jermaine's adjoining cabin that the guard wasn't standing in front of the suite's main entrance.

My heart fell because I was busted anyway. They had gone into the suite for something and discovered me gone. Dammit, I couldn't catch a break. Despite the futility of it, we went in through Jermaine's door anyway. Neither Jermaine nor I had said anything, but the look he gave me when we saw the guard was gone said everything.

'What do we do?' Jermaine asked when we were inside his cabin and the door was shut.

Barbie spoke first, 'I think Patricia is long overdue a workout. Shall we deal with that first. You did so well to avoid the unhealthy food and the alcohol. You should reward your body with a hard-cardio session.'

I laughed. I couldn't help it. I felt like I had burned a thousand calories just walking around in the heat today. Sure, why not, let's get a workout in before they clap me in irons. The humour didn't last long though, there was all too much harsh reality bearing down on me.

I took Jermaine's hand. 'I think I should get clean and get changed and wait for them to come for me. We can say that you were oblivious to my absence because you were dismissed by me this morning and went ashore. I see no reason why they wouldn't believe that. There is no need for you to take the heat for helping me.'

I could see he wanted to protest – a natural human reaction, but I wasn't going to let him get into trouble for me. I should never have involved him.

'I'm going for a shower,' I announced, letting go of his hand before he could say anything and pushing open the door that led into my kitchen.

At which point I screamed.

Jermaine and Barbie rushed to my side, Barbie appearing to my left, Jermaine on my right and the shock of the sight in front of me caused them to both scream as well.

The reason the guard wasn't outside my door was because he was in my kitchen with a knife buried to the hilt in his ear. He looked very, very dead.

When my heart started beating again, and I was able to take a couple of breaths, I knelt to examine him.

Behind me Barbie was saying, 'Oh, my God,' over and over and over.

Who had done this? Why had they done it? I wouldn't mind knowing *how* as well. I was careful not to touch anything, but now I had a big problem. It was clear the man had been dead for a while - the blood from the wound was dry on his skin and on the collar of his white shirt.

What did this mean?

'I have to get cleaned up,' I announced, trying to think logically through what we needed to do now. 'Barbie,' I called her name, but she didn't react. Her eyes were locked on the terrible sight in my kitchen.

'Barbie!' My raised voice to penetrate her shock, her head and eyes snapping around to show me how scared she felt.

I softened my tone again. 'Sweetie, you need to go back to your cabin or to the gym.' Her scared eyes dictated I needed to say more. 'Jermaine will come for you later. Jermaine will be able to claim that he was off the boat today and returned to find the body. I will say that I was in my bedroom and knew nothing about it. They won't believe me, but they already think I am a killer.' It was a hasty plan and full of holes, but it was all I could come up with on the spot.

Neither Barbie nor Jermaine moved. 'Quickly, guys,' I implored. 'We know that none of us is the killer, so we have to trust each other.'

Barbie managed to mumble, 'Okay.'

As I stepped around the outstretched legs of the dead guard, I saw Jermaine and Barbie hug and air kiss. Then Barbie was gone.

I couldn't believe this was happening to me: dead bodies stacking up, international jewel theft, staying in the royal suite. It was overwhelming and exhilarating at the same time, but the thing I really couldn't believe, was that I, Patricia Fisher, was handling it. I was taking charge and moving forward and doing things that two days ago I would have told the world I couldn't do.

I was about to go for a shower while a dead body sat on the deck in my cabin for goodness sake.

I felt like James Bond.

I placed the call to ship's security myself once I was dressed and had given myself a little time to think about what I wanted to say. I was determined to sail as close to the truth as I could while also lying through my teeth.

Just a shade more than five minutes later, Commander Schooner burst through the door to my apartment and began accusing me of my second murder.

'How did you lure Lieutenant Davis inside?' Schooner raged, 'It couldn't have been for sex.'

I felt sure his comment was intended to be an insult, not a claim that the dead guard was homosexual.

'Commander Schooner,' I started, keeping my voice as even and emotionless as possible. 'I will say this again and I am going to ask you to listen even though I am certain you won't do so: I am not the killer.'

'Ha!' he scoffed. 'So someone else lured him into your room and murdered him while you were doing … what?'

'Sleeping.' I provided a lie they couldn't disprove and didn't rely on anyone else to have to also lie.

Commander Schooner turned to face me. His features set to a murderous expression, and all aimed at yours truly.

'You invite me to believe that a large, muscular man was murdered in your suite, and you slept through the event, only discovering him many hours later. How long's he been dead, Doc?' he called over his shoulder to where a small Chinese man with a doctor's bag was examining the body.

I could only see the man's feet sticking out from the behind the kitchen counter, but his voice came back, 'I would say three hours, maybe a little more given the body temperature.'

'Three hours,' Commander Schooner repeated. 'And you were asleep all that time in the middle of the day?'

Instead of answering, I pointed out something Commander Schooner had yet to notice. 'The man's body is hidden from view.'

'Huh?'

I was sitting in one of the sumptuous high-backed armchairs while Commander Schooner paced about in his agitated, angry state. I had chosen to sit when I made the call to summon security and hadn't left the chair since. Honestly, I was feeling a little weak from it all. I had a dead body in my kitchen for goodness sake.

I lifted an arm and pointed across to the kitchen. 'The poor man is hidden by the kitchen counter. One had to go not only into the kitchen but then around to the other side of the counter to find him. When I woke, as always, there was water laid out for me because my butler is attentive. I had no reason to go into the kitchen until a few seconds before I called you.'

'What made you go into the kitchen then?' Commander Schooner immediately tried to pick holes in my story.

'I was getting peckish. Confined to my suite, I refused to let the same fate befall my butler, so I sent him ashore with his friends. When I got hungry, I went into the kitchen to find some fruit or a sandwich, which I still haven't had because I am falsely imprisoned and have to wonder if I might be next to get murdered.' I made a point of saying the words *falsely imprisoned* at twice the volume to show my indignation.

131

If Schooner even heard it, he showed no sign. Instead, he all but grinned at me, a knowing look that tried to say he wasn't fooled for a second.

'I'm quite sure that if the killer were able to take out your guard but you were the intended target, you would by now be quite dead.' He had me there. 'Yet again, Mrs Fisher, you have no alibi and yet again I am not able to unequivocally prove your guilt. Rest assured though, the murder weapon will be taken as evidence, and all of this will be handed over to the police in St Kitts when we arrive.'

'Why not Madeira?' I asked, genuinely curious.

He frowned at me. 'Hmmm?'

'You said I would be handed over to the police in St Kitts. Why not do it here in Madeira?'

He turned to look right at me, fixing me with a hard stare. 'Because I was being good to you, Mrs Fisher. You should thank me for it. There is no British consulate in Madeira and the native language is not English. It will be much easier for you to arrange legal counsel in St Kitts. Don't worry though, you will be in jail soon enough.'

'Will that be all?' It was my turn to fix him with my own hard stare. 'I'm still the innocent party, Commander Schooner. I'm still the guest held prisoner in the royal suite on the world's largest luxury ocean liner because you cannot look far enough beyond your own ego to see that I am not the killer. What possible gain could there be for me in that man's death?'

Commander Schooner came across the room at me, his face an angry, rage-filled sneer. 'That is what I intend to find out,' he snarled mere inches from my face as his proximity forced me back into the headrest of the chair.

Then he turned on his heel and stormed from the room, yelling, 'Double the guard and bring me her butler,' as he went out.

Poor Jermaine would be grilled about his involvement, his whereabouts today, and probably about my movements as well. Luckily, I was convinced that Commander Schooner didn't have any notion that Jermaine was my accomplice. It seemed more likely that Schooner wanted to talk to Jermaine so that he could be engaged to act as a spy to report on me.

I was fine with that.

My stomach growled meaningfully. The lunch Barbie bullied me into ordering in Funchal was long gone, but I didn't think I could order food to the room just yet since there was still a dead body in the kitchen. I didn't want to summon Jermaine to bring me something either because he would have to step over the body and the men taking care of it to get to me.

Odd though it might sound, the most logical option I could come up with was to call Barbie to take me to the gym. She would ensure I didn't train on an empty stomach at least.

True to his word, there were now two guards outside my door when Barbie and I left to go to the gym, which they emptied in deference to my visit. They also arranged two more guards to come to the gym with me.

The meat-headed, crewcut-wearing, silent sentinels lifted heavy weights in one corner, never taking their eyes off me although I had to wonder if they were, in fact, staring at Barbie instead and lifting the weights in a bid to impress her.

Thankfully, upon hearing that I hadn't eaten, Barbie provided me with a meal replacement shake that she claimed contained all the nutrients I needed, and then insisted I perform a very slow warm up for thirty minutes so I didn't immediately bring the shake back up.

It wasn't that much of a reprieve.

An hour of sustained cardio on about eight different machines reduced me to a wobbly-kneed, sopping wet, sweaty mess and now I really needed something more substantial than a thick milkshake to eat.

Dripping onto the mat, with the two guards across the room trying hard to not show their disgust, I looked up as Barbie sat herself cross legged in front of me.

'We just need to do some warm down exercises now,' she said.

'Really? We're not finished yet?' I panted, stopping short of pleading but not far short.

Barbie smiled at me. 'This is the easy bit and will stop your muscles stiffening and feeling sore when you wake up.' In her hand she held a remote. When she pointed it across the room, relaxing music began to play.

I suspected that nothing short of sleeping for two weeks would prevent my muscles from feeling stiff when I woke up. However, after ten minutes of stretching my arms, legs, back, shoulders and all my other bits, I had to admit that I felt better. I had also stopped sweating, though I was no less of a sweaty mess than before.

Barbie was something of a miracle worker when it came to fitness. Not that I was claiming to have suddenly turned my life around or dropped twenty pounds, but I did feel mentally refreshed and buoyed by surviving the workouts. She was harsh but she was encouraging, and she made me feel good about the effort I was putting in.

'I need to eat.'

'That is exactly what I need you to do, Patty' she agreed with me. 'Your body needs to be refuelled now. Remember, food is fuel. When you are hungry it wants nutrients not calories. I will be along to your room with a meal shortly.'

'Don't I get to pick?' I asked a little sulkily.

She paused midway through getting up. 'What would you pick?'

Meeting her gaze, I had to reply with, 'Whatever you told me I was allowed to eat.'

'Super.' Barbie bounced onto her feet, told the guards we were leaving, and brought me a towel to mop up the pool of sweat surrounding me. I am so sexy.

The guards were just finishing up and tidying away the equipment they'd used. One of them coughed when I got too close to the door – a polite warning to stay where they could see me.

Waiting for them to be ready to escort me back to my suite, I poked around by the door, looking at safety notices and signs because my eyes had to look at something.

The gym staff - there were four listed - all had an eight by ten photograph of their smiling head and torso. Their names were listed beneath in each case. Barbie's real name was Barbara. Oddly, it hadn't occurred to me that Barbie was an abridgement.

When the guards finally decided they were ready to take me back to my cabin, sauntering across the gym toward me, I gave them a smile. It was out of place given the situation I found myself in, but I also knew it was not what they expected, and I wanted to keep as many people off balance as possible.

In the passageway outside the gym, they fell into place either side of me, remaining silent as we walked back around the corner and some one hundred yards to my door.

This was my third day on the Aurelia and so far I had seen about half of one percent of it. I couldn't decide if I were desperate to clear my name so I could leave and never come back or so I could get on and explore the place.

I went to Madeira today for heaven's sake and never made it out of the dock. Would I ever get the chance to come back? That I finally visited a place I'd only heard about or seen on TV and got not the slightest chance to look around seemed so unfair. It was as if the universe had chosen to conspire against me and thwart my every plan.

At the door to my suite were two more hard-looking men in uniform. They both looked like they were ex-military and maybe they were. All four of them eyed me with suspicious contempt as if trying to intimidate me. It was working.

With all four sets of eyes boring into me while I waited for them to open the door and show me inside, I managed to quietly squeak, 'I didn't kill your friend.'

None of them replied to my comment, but the one who opened the door said, 'Very good, madam,' in a deep throaty tone.

When the door closed behind me and I was inside my suite once more, I breathed a sigh of relief. It wasn't much, but I felt a little safer tucked away in my cabin.

Barbie would be along soon enough, but there were things I needed to do before I ate, one of which was to get a shower. I put my bag down, kicked off my running shoes in the suite's little lobby area and turned around.

The unexpected presence looming in the doorway through to my suite almost made me wet myself.

'Can I assist you with anything, madam?'

Yet again his silent approach caught me off guard, stopping my heart because I wasn't expecting it. With one hand against the wall to keep me upright, I gritted my teeth at him, 'Dammit, Jermaine. You have got to learn to make some noise as you walk.'

'My apologies, madam. Is there anything I can help you with?'

I walked toward my bedroom, thinking about all the things I wanted to do. It surprised me, with all the other stuff whizzing around in my head, that it was Charlie who made it to the top of my list.

'I need to get access to a phone so I can call my husband. I don't think ...' then I trailed off what I was saying. I had already involved Jermaine too deeply. 'I could really do with using a phone,' I finished meekly.

Jermaine made an apologetic face. 'I'm afraid Commander Schooner was very insistent that you not be permitted any internet enabled devices. He believes you will communicate with your accomplices, or perhaps a fence for the stolen jewellery. I am under threat of dismissal if I assist you any further.'

I nodded, 'I understand. I am sorry for the trouble this has caused you.'

He inclined his head toward me in acknowledgement, 'My instructions are to report your activities to Commander Schooner.' I could hear the regret in his voice.

'You must do what is necessary, Jermaine. I promise I will try to cause you no more problems.'

'Is there anything else I can help you with, madam?'

I shook my head, trying to limit what I said for fear that my anger might spill out in Jermaine's direction. He didn't deserve to be spoken to harshly by anyone, let alone me.

'I just need a shower for now, thank you, Jermaine.' With that I began pulling my top off as I went into my bedroom and closed the door.

When I came back out into the suite's main living area twenty minutes later, my hair still damp and threatening to turn into a puff ball if left unchecked, I found Jermaine on my sun terrace. He had my food and was ready to serve.

'Good evening, madam,' he greeted me.

'Really, Jermaine? We snuck off the ship, pretended to be fortune tellers and then you smuggled me back on to then find a dead body in my kitchen. Must we pretend I am a princess when it is just the two of us?'

138

He looked slightly horrified. 'Decorum dictates, madam.'

I rolled my eyes and let him pour my water. It was sparkling, what a treat.

Barbie dropped off my food while I was getting clean but did not wait around to speak with me. There was no reason for her to do so, I was just some mad old woman with a noose around her neck. She was being as helpful as she could. They both were.

Staring out to sea with my butler standing impassive and still just a few feet away, I realised that with all I had going on, Charlie had barely made it into my thoughts today at any point.

What did that say about me? About our marriage? Admittedly, the events of the day had proven to be quite distracting, but I felt... what? Lonely?

No more than I had the last few years.

What then? I couldn't decide, but as I tucked into an exquisite sea bass on a bed of fennel with a passionfruit sauce, I wondered what was happening to me. There were changes occurring, both to my life and to my personality. I felt as if I were on the brink of an epiphany and had to wonder if the biggest changes were in the way I viewed the world.

It had been a long day and I was tired, yet there was something itching at the back of my head. It was something I had seen but I couldn't quite connect the dots to work out what it was or what it meant.

I needed to find out more about Jack Langley, but I also wanted to investigate Neil Hammond AKA Flint Magnum. I wasn't satisfied with the reason he gave for his presence on the ship. Also, what was with

Commander Schooner? He knew about Flint Magnum and thus knew Jack Langley was probably the jewel thief they were looking for.

Why hadn't Schooner been able to move on Jack sooner or search the man's suite while he was ashore or being entertained somewhere. It seemed like a simple thing to do, but maybe he had already done so and hadn't been able to find what he was looking for. Maybe the jewels had been securely stashed in Jack's safe. Or maybe there were no jewels.

Later, as I settled down to sleep, I was kept awake by the number of things I didn't know. How was I ever going to prove my innocence if I couldn't work out what was going on?

Just as I was dropping off my eyes snapped open, and I flew from my bed.

'Where is it?' I asked the air as I rummaged through my drawers and the detritus of bits and pieces on the dressing table. Just when I was about to call Jermaine, I spotted it.

Snatching it up, I turned it over in my fingers and flicked on a light so I could read it. Flint Magnum didn't drop a bank card, the business card I found was his.

I dismissed it at the time because the name I expected to see wasn't the one on it. It never got a second thought, and when I emptied my pockets that night, it went into a drawer with everything else. It had been there ever since.

'Patricia, this is a clue,' I said to myself, tapping the card on my fingernails.

It was a typical business card designed to fit neatly into the slot in one's wallet or purse. The name on it was Samuel Lawrence and he worked for Axiz International Insurance Brokers. The title displayed below the name was Recovery Agent.

I wasn't sure what the job entailed but my guess would be that after an insurance firm paid out for insured losses, the recovery agent then tried to recover what had been lost. Did that make sense? I wasn't sure, but then I had no idea who Samuel Lawrence was. I saw Flint Magnum drop something.

Was it this card?

It was bedtime and I was tired and though I crawled back into bed imagining that the million questions tumbling around inside my head would keep me awake, they didn't.

Sunlight pierced my eyes as I sat up in bed to welcome the day. 'Good morning, madam,' Jermaine greeted me as he finished perfecting the way the curtains hung. 'Miss Berkeley is waiting for you in the living room.'

I blinked a couple of times.

'Okay?' I hazarded while my brain tried to catch up. As the fog of sleep lifted away, I remembered asking Jermaine what time Barbie would be available in the morning. I felt bad they had to empty the upper deck gym of everyone else every time I wanted to use it. Going to bed early and sober last night, it seemed like a good idea to get in there at the crack of dawn today before the crowd of crazy fitness fanatics arrived.

It didn't feel like such a good idea now and despite Barbie's reassurance that warming down correctly would prevent my body from stiffening, I felt like I'd been getting amorous with a walrus last night.

'Coffee,' I begged.

'Very good, madam.'

As Jermaine scuttled off to fetch some go-juice, I settled back down into my cloud-like goose-down pillows. Maybe Barbie would be happy to wait.

Wait a second! Her name isn't Barbie it's Barbara! She shortened it, or people shortened it for her because that's what people do.

That's why I didn't find Jack Langley when I looked for him! His name isn't Jack at all!

It would be James or John or something like that. Or maybe Jack was a preferred middle name. My eyes now wide open, I sprang from my bed, slipped on the mat, and fell on my backside. I guess I made a racket because Jermaine and Barbie both peered around the doorframe the next second.

'Everything alright, madam?' my butler politely enquired.

'I figured it out!' I was getting myself up awkwardly from the carpet, my flannel pyjamas tangling around my feet. 'Jack isn't his real name, it's an abridgement! I need to get to a computer.'

Jermaine and Barbie were still standing in the doorway when I got there, their faces both set to a quizzical O shape. I tried to explain myself a little better.

'Jack Langley. His first name isn't Jack, but it might be John or James. Chances are he kept his initial, but it could be that Jack is his second name.' Words were spilling from my mouth in a torrent. The itchy thing at the back of my skull was going nuts – I was onto something, and I needed to chase it down now or I might just explode.

Jermaine nodded his head in understanding. 'The computer might be tough,' said Jermaine with some regret. 'Commander Schooner had it disabled.'

Yeah, he did that, I remembered. Combined with confiscating my phone, it was why I hadn't been able to talk to my husband in two days. Not that I had any idea what to say to him, but right now Charlie was the least of my worries.

As if Jermaine was reading my thoughts, he said, 'Madam, I know I said yesterday that I couldn't help you, but I laid awake half the night feeling guilty about it. I believe you are innocent – certainly the second murder was not by your hand, so I am going to help you in whatever way I can. Commander Schooner and his … men,' he picked the word carefully, clearly considering that another word might be more appropriate, 'confiscated my phone as well so I could not be tempted to lend it to you, but I have always had an old backup one. I charged it last night.'

It was a generous offer, but I didn't want to confuse my head further by getting my husband involved in this mess. 'Thank you, Jermaine. I don't need to call anyone right now.'

A confused look washed across his face, 'No, I mean. You can use it to look on the internet, madam.'

'I can?' Now it was my turn to look confused. Barbie was fishing her phone out of a snug pocket on the hip of her skin-tight leggings. 'I mean, I guess I know that phones can do that, but I don't know how to do that with them.' Did my phone do that?

Like a Neanderthal standing before advanced beings, I watched as their thumbs flashed about. 'J-A-M-E-S L-A-N-G-L-E-Y,' Jermaine spelt to Barbie. Half a second later they were both showing me their tiny screens.

The chase was on again.

The elation I felt at that moment, didn't last long as we quickly worked through as many permutations of his name as we could without getting a result. Disappointed, I returned Jermaine's phone.

'So, what now?' Barbie wanted to know. 'Shall we go to the gym?'

Dear Lord, no.

'How about if we looked for just his last name and combine it with words like jewel thief or convicted? Would that work?' I asked hopefully.

Jermaine shrugged, 'It might.'

More flashing fingers. They were sat side by side on the couch in my living area, with me pacing in front of them nervously. In truth, I realised more than a day ago that I was clutching at straws in my search for the man. If I assume Jack Langley really was a jewel thief then what did that tell me? I still wouldn't know who killed him or why. I doubted I would ever discover the first thing about him. And what if he had never been caught? There would be no record of him, surely?

Pacing and trying hard to not bite my nails, it almost made me jump when Barbie blurted, 'Oh.'

I turned to find her staring at her phone and Jermaine leaning in to see what was on her screen.

'Barbie has found something interesting about a jewel thief,' Jermaine began reading, 'Shaun Metcalf was convicted of the theft of the Sapphire of Zangrabar when his fingers were found at the scene. Mr Metcalf, thirty-seven, denies having an accomplice, but the jewel was never recovered, and Interpol argue that he could not have gained access or escaped from the New York Geological Society, where it was on display, by himself. Despite his wounds, he evaded the authorities and was arrested two days later when his wounds were matched to a police report.' Jermaine sat back again and looked up at me. 'It goes on to say that he was jailed for fifteen years. It's an old newspaper article.' He gave Barbie a questioning look. 'I don't see a reference to anyone called Langley.'

I scrunched my forehead in misunderstanding. 'Barbie, what made you jump when you saw the article?'

She looked up. 'Because of the picture of Shaun.'

That added no clarity at all. 'What about him?' I asked.

Barbie smiled her usual sweet smile. 'He's in the cabin next to mine. He's really nice.'

Jermaine and I stared at each other. The presence of another jewel thief on board just couldn't be a coincidence. 'Can I see?' I held out my hand for Barbie to pass me her phone, but she got up instead and came to stand next to me, doing something complex with her fingers to make the photograph fill the screen.

A chill ran down my spine. I knew the man. He was younger in the picture, but the same scar I noted when he first smiled at me ran through a younger eyebrow and onto the cheek below.

'I need to speak with the captain,' I murmured. 'Can you arrange that?' Jermaine looked unsure. 'This man carried my luggage when I came on board,' I explained. 'He has to be Jack's killer. There's too much coincidence.'

Jermaine nodded his understanding. 'I'll see what I can do, madam.' He left via his usual door to avoid the guards outside the suite's main entrance.

Barbie was left behind with me. 'What else does it say?' I asked.

'Oh, ah, here.' She handed me her phone, which immediately went to a different screen the moment I touched it. I made a grunting noise and showed her as I handed it back. She touched it again and the screen with Shaun Metcalf's face was back.

It was a guilty face if ever I saw one, the scar on his eyebrow no doubt the product of a shady past or a delinquent childhood. The captain would have to pay attention to me now that I could identify a convicted jewel thief among his crew. I continued reading the old news article, but it didn't say anywhere that he was a known accomplice of anyone called

146

Langley. However, it did say that he was from Brooklyn, the same place Jack admitted he grew up.

I handed the phone back to Barbie. 'Can you search for more information about the missing jewel and any suspects?'

She said, 'Okay,' with her usual sweet grin and almost instantly handed the phone back to me with the results. Again, I touched it and killed the screen I was looking at. 'Like this.' Barbie patiently showed me how to touch the screen and move it about without making it go away.

Having mastered that, I discovered there were numerous articles about the jewel the scar-faced murderer was accused of stealing. It would take hours to read them all. Time I didn't have as Jermaine would return any moment with the captain. 'Is it possible to narrow the search?' I asked.

'Sure. What do you want to look for?'

'Can you combine the name of the jewel with Jack Langley or just Langley?' She could and she did, this time getting only one article, in which it named Shaun Metcalf as having several potential accomplices.

It was an old piece, written more than a decade ago, but it listed four different men that were known to Shaun Metcalf. Any of them could have been the other man the police suspected to be involved in the jewel theft. Actually, it said that it could have been one or all of them but went on to advise the reader that two had been eliminated as unlikely because they were in jail now and another had been questioned by the police and released. It left a man called John Langley and it provided a picture. He and Metcalf served jail time together in their twenties for stealing jewellery.

147

The picture was of a man in his twenties, but it was the same Jack Langley I met on my first night. I had found him. There was no doubt in my mind that Shaun Metcalf took a job on the ship to get even with his old partner. He murdered Jack Langley and took the jewels Flint Magnum believed Jack had.

Find him and the case was solved. I would be free finally.

A loud knock at the door broke my concentration and heralded it opening. It wasn't the captain that preceded Jermaine into the room though, it was the ever-unpleasant Commander Schooner once more. He already had a sneer on his lips. An embarrassed Jermaine shuffled in behind him, a burly guard on his shoulder like a threat.

'Can I help you, Mrs Fisher? Your butler seems to think you have evidence that might prove your innocence.' He made no attempt to hide the derision in his voice.

I turned to Barbie to ask for her phone again. 'May I?' She willingly handed it over. 'This person,' I showed Schooner the screen, 'is a member of the crew, a convicted jewel thief, and a known accomplice of the man we know as Jack Langley. Jack Langley's real first name is John.'

He looked down at the phone but then back up at me before he had time to take anything in. He looked angry. Really angry.

'You gave her a phone?' he snapped at Barbie. She flinched under his verbal assault, her perfect features now contorted in shock. 'I gave strict instruction that Mrs Fisher was not to have communication with the outside world. You can expect to lose your job for this.'

'What are you doing?' I demanded. 'This man is the killer.' I had the phone up to his face so he couldn't avoid it. 'He went to jail when he and Jack stole a priceless jewel. The jewel was never recovered but Shaun

Metcalf was convicted for the theft while his partner got away. He is on board to exact his revenge. I bet if you search his room, you will find the missing jewels. This is the man who killed Lieutenant Davis.'

Commander Schooner's attention was all on me, his face mere inches from mine. He didn't say anything for a couple of seconds, then he cracked a smile and began to laugh. Barbie's horrified expression slowly relaxed. She was hoping his threat of dismissal was somehow part of a joke she didn't understand. A grin flitted nervously across her face. I was just utterly bewildered.

Before I could ask what he found so funny, he started speaking, 'You do have a wonderful imagination, Mrs Fisher. Jewel thieves, accomplices, old convicts getting revenge on their partners after spending years in jail harbouring a secret. How do you come up with it all?' He was still laughing between sentences, a small tear escaping his left eye from the mirth.

'This is evidence,' I pointed out, waving the phone around under his nose. However, the certainty I felt a minute ago was slipping away.

'It's nothing,' he replied. 'Circumstantial coincidence at best.' He took the hat he held under his right arm and placed it back on his head, turning to a mirror across the room to check his reflection. 'Will there be anything else?'

I stared at him, utterly lost again. I thought I had a solution. Would the captain have listened? When I said nothing, because I could think of nothing to say, Commander Schooner tilted his head in a mocking salute and left my suite.

Pausing at the door, he had a final comment for Jermaine and Barbie, 'You can both consider yourselves suspended pending formal review. I want you out of this room in the next two minutes or I will have the guards remove you. Don't expect to keep your jobs once we reach St Kitts.' Then he closed the door and was gone.

'I'm fired?' Barbie said slowly as if trying the concept out to see how it felt.

Jermaine settled onto the nearest couch. The words, 'Oh my,' escaped his lips.

I felt terrible. How had it all come to this?

'The captain wouldn't come,' said Jermaine from his seated position. 'I found him, but Commander Schooner was there too. As soon as I said what I needed the captain for, he insisted it was Commander Schooner's business. There was nothing I could do.'

'This isn't your fault,' I replied instantly.

Jermaine looked up at me, an incredulous look on his face.

'Of course it's not my fault. I haven't done anything.' He was getting angry now. 'This is your fault, but I still seem to be out of a job.' He stood up to deliver the outburst, then looked embarrassed once the words left his mouth. 'Sorry, madam, I'm...' He didn't finish the sentence. He just turned and left, exiting the room via the door in the kitchen to get back to his cabin.

I turned to Barbie, my expression wretched.

She spoke first, 'I should go.' Tears were not far from falling, the words came out around a barely suppressed sob. I handed back her phone and she left too.

All alone in my vast suite, I felt like I had to be the most miserable person on the planet. I had no friends, I had no husband, I had nowhere to live once I got off this ship, but that was probably a moot point because I was accused of murder and was most likely going directly to jail. Even if I were eventually proven innocent, I would still spend time in a cell while I waited for a trial.

I crumpled to the deck, too stunned to walk to the bedroom to collapse on the bed and somehow too miserable to cry. In my depression, I had to ask if I would simply be better off jumping from the balcony right now. It would be so easy to do. The doors were only a few feet away. I got to my feet, wobbling on uncertain legs as I made my way across the room. As I put my hand on the chrome handle to let myself outside, the door behind me opened.

A voice said, 'I have to make sure you are alone.'

I looked at my hand on the door handle and snatched it away, horrified that I was genuinely contemplating suicide.

'What the heck am I doing?'

From behind me the voice said, 'Huh?'

I turned to see a guard in the doorway. He was looking at me with a confused look.

'Where are they?' he asked.

Time to play dumb. 'Where's who?'

He met me with a disbelieving look, I was wasting his time and he knew it.

'Your butler and the gym bunny. Where are they? I must escort them out. Commander Schooner's orders.'

'They left already.'

'Left? But I'm guarding the door.' Then I saw the light dawn. For three days they had been guarding the door to my suite to prevent me from leaving, but my butler had his own entrance.

The guard in his pristine white uniform looked across the suite to the kitchen and the door that led out of it.

'Mike!' the man yelled to his partner outside. Mike poked his head around the suite's main entrance door as the first man advanced across the room toward the kitchen.

'What?' asked Mike.

His partner was now in the kitchen. 'I think there is another way out of this suite. Get over here!'

Curious, Mike went to join his partner, both going through the door into Jermaine's cabin and leaving the main door to my suite open and unattended.

I glanced quickly at Jermaine's door. They were both inside his cabin. 'I'll just let myself out then,' I whispered to myself as I crossed the room, grabbing my handbag and a baseball cap as I went. Then, still in my pyjamas and slippers and running like the devil himself was behind me, I went in search of Shaun Metcalf.

Running was going to draw attention but hanging around in the passageway outside my suite didn't seem like a good idea either, so I did my best to combine a nonchalant stroll with speed walking and hurried away as fast as I could.

When I heard a string of swear words coming from the open door of the suite, I abandoned any notion of being surreptitious and ran as fast as my little legs would take me.

The guards had realised their error and were giving chase!

Before they could get out of my cabin and spot me, I made the corner and ducked out of view. I wasn't out of earshot though and could hear them blaming each other while exchanging some inventive expletives.

They only had two choices for which direction I might have gone, so even though they came across as a little dumb, they would catch me soon enough if I hung around. There was an elevator bank to my right, the lights above both showed neither car was on my level.

Were they on their way up? I stabbed the button between the two elevators repeatedly even though I knew doing so wouldn't make the doors open any sooner. I wanted to skip back to the corner and see if the guards were coming but if they were, I would probably scream and wet myself.

The left-hand car was clawing its way toward the upper deck, the number shown above it slowly ticking inexorably through the teens.

I heard running footsteps. Heavy boots echoing in the passageway that led to my suite.

The guards checked one direction, failed to find me there, and were now heading straight for me!

Stuff waiting for the elevator, I started for the stairs. But the second I got moving, the elevator pinged. Split with indecision, I flipped a mental coin and dived through the silver doors as they swished opened. Throwing myself inside, I slammed into the far wall just as both guards came barrelling around the corner.

They saw me instantly, pointing and yelling as they sprinted toward the closing doors.

Caught inside the confines of the steel box, I had nowhere to go and couldn't have got there if I did. The doors slid shut in the nick of time, the guards' bodies slamming against them and rattling the elevator as it started to move. I wanted to breathe a sigh of relief, but I wasn't certain the elevator would descend faster than they could get down the stairs.

Yet again, I was trapped.

I forced myself to consider options. Is it better to go all the way to the bottom and hope you outrun them or get off on a random deck and see what happens? Surely, the farther I went or the longer I was in the elevator, the more likely it was that they would meet a barrier of some kind that would slow them down. That was my plan then.

I didn't know what deck Barbie's cabin was on, only that it was somewhere in the bowels of the ship. I would take the elevator to deck seven where it terminated and get off there. I would need a different elevator or some stairs to access the crew decks. However, I was convinced it wouldn't take me long to find a man that could tell me where the super-sexy, toned, athletic, blonde girl lived.

154

I hadn't considered one important factor in my plan though: other people could press the elevator call button. Two decks down, the car slowed, stopped, and opened. A nice-looking couple in their sixties were waiting to get in. They looked a little surprised at my ready-for-bed outfit but smiled pleasantly as they joined me.

'Thirteen, please,' the lady requested since I was standing next to the buttons.

Across the atrium in which the elevator opened, a stairwell door burst open, spewing the two guards.

They were a little out of breath, but when they saw me framed inside the elevator car, they grinned like foxes in a chicken coop. I was a rabbit in headlights again, stabbing the button and trying not to wet myself.

'Shouldn't we wait for those men?' the lady asked, her face genuinely confused by my desperation to get the doors shut. She raised her arm to stop the doors as they started to shut.

I yelled, 'Noooo!' as I slammed into her, pushing her to the side of the car and watching in relief as the doors shut on the guards' angry faces once more.

'Is everything alright?' the man asked as he pulled his wife gently away from me.

God, I must look like a crazy woman.

'I'm sorry,' I blurted. 'So, so sorry. Those men are chasing me, I just need to get away.'

'Goodness,' the wife said, her hand to her heart in shock. 'Why?'

Why? I stared at them, my mouth open, struggling to find something to say.

The lift pinged again, the doors opened to my left, and I bolted, leaving the couples' startled faces behind as I crossed the atrium as fast as I could go in my slippers.

How far behind were the guards? I wasn't even sure what number deck I was on now, but details could wait until I was safe. I reached the door that led from the elevator atrium onto the deck itself and suddenly found myself outside in the sun. There was a pool in front of me and despite the early hour there were children playing in it and a stack of adults lying on the sun loungers around it.

Should I risk a look back into the elevator area to see if the guards were there? Probably not a clever idea. Instead, I forced myself to stroll nonchalantly by all the people enjoying the early morning sunshine. They barely noticed me even with my odd choice of clothes.

I reached the far side of the pool, ducked behind a bar, and found my way back into the ship more than a hundred yards from where I emerged without hearing anyone shouting for me to stop or raising an alarm. I gave myself a minute at that point to lean against a handy wall.

The ship was too vast for them to find me. At least that's what I told myself as I set off again. It was too big and there were too many people for them to be able to catch me unless they got lucky.

However, the problem I faced now was that I had no idea where I was on the ship or where I was trying to get to - two pieces of information one might think vital for navigation. When I crossed the deck outside, there were perhaps six decks above me reaching up toward the blue sky. If I estimated that there are twenty decks - the captain told me how many there were on the first day, but I hadn't been paying attention - then I have fourteen decks beneath me, and Barbie is toward the bottom of them. I was willing to bet there were maps or pictorial layouts all over the ship, but do you think I could find one now that I was in desperate need?

What I came to first was another wide, open area filled with people. It contained shops and signs for a cinema. Escalators dropped down to the next level where I could see a water fountain surrounded by chairs set up to look like an Italian village square. Most of the chairs were occupied with passengers eating their breakfast as wait staff in bright red shirts delivered food and collected empty plates. It looked wonderful. I had so much of this ship that I wanted to explore if I ever got the chance.

I rode the escalator down, taking it all in, sniffing the glorious smells of coffee and fresh bread that filled the air. My stomach grumbled its emptiness because breakfast got skipped yet again and I had to fight an inner demon who argued I could stop for food now - the guards would never find me here.

I doubted I would feel safe, so my hunger went unanswered for now. Crossing the open space, I spotted a male member of the wait staff and waved to get his attention.

'Good morning, madam. Welcome to La Trevita. Please take a seat anywhere and someone will be along momentarily to take your order.' It was all delivered with practised polish and a slight French accent despite the Italian setting.

'Thank you. I was hoping you might be able to help me with something else though.' His eyebrows twitched as he waited for me to continue. 'I am looking for a friend of mine, she's my gym instructor, Barbie Berkeley. She's a member of the crew. Could you direct me to the crew accommodation, please?'

157

The young man looked surprised at the question but provided an answer anyway, 'The crew are mostly located on deck four.'

'Deck four, thank you.' I turned to go but he called me back.

'You will not be able to access it though. The crew areas are separate from the passenger areas.'

'How do I get to her then?'

He sort of shrugged. 'I guess you can go to one of the entry doors and ask for her. There's an elevator that will take you there on the next deck. Take the stairs on the port side.' He chuckled graciously at my confused face and pointed which way to go.

I set off, hurrying but not running and hoping not only that I could follow his directions but also find someone that would help me locate Barbie when I got there.

His directions were spot on, thankfully, which meant I found the stairs I needed easily. At the bottom there were two members of crew waiting for the elevator - a chef and a man in a grubby maintenance outfit complete with toolbelt. No doubt there were myriad items that needed fixing or maintaining.

As I approached, the chef turned his head slightly to see who it was and did a double take when he saw my face.

It was Ian, the chef I had made sushi with on the second night while trying to catch Flint Magnum.

'Hi,' I waved.

He frowned, perplexed by my outfit. 'Did you forget to get dressed?'

Thinking quickly, I said, 'I just nipped up to my kitchen to check on an icing sculpture I made last night. I was nervous it might have sagged, and I would need to get started again now. It looks okay though.' The chefs put lots of artistic touches to the food presentation, I hadn't seen a table yet that didn't have a masterpiece carved from fruit or moulded from butter.

Ian accepted my answer with a disinterested nod and turned back to the elevator just as the doors opened. 'You certainly have it easier on deck eighteen. Chef Schneider would never tolerate any of us stepping foot in his kitchen in less than full uniform.'

We all stepped inside where I watched Ian use a key card to activate the buttons. The elevator wouldn't go anywhere unless the person getting on had one. This was where I expected to get stopped and have to ask someone to fetch Barbie, but Ian thought I was just another member of the crew.

I pushed my luck a little further. 'Do you know where Barbie Berkeley's cabin is? She is going to help me with weight management.' I picked a believable lie.

'I do,' the maintenance man said, a leering grin creeping onto his face without invitation. He saw my expression and quickly reset his expression. 'I can show you if you like.'

'Super, thanks.' This was going better than I could have hoped for.

The elevator pinged again, and we all got off. I was the last one on so was nearest the doors when they opened but not knowing where I was supposed to be going, I hesitated, causing both men to bump into me as they moved forward.

'Sorry. Daydreaming again,' I apologised.

Ian shook his head as he walked away.

'This way,' said the maintenance guy, hooking a finger for me to follow.

The deck we were on was vast and there was no natural light. I wondered if we were now below the water line, a thought that made me feel a bit odd. Would I be happy in the bottom of the ship? Memories of watching *Titanic* at the cinema surfaced – the sinky bits in particular - as the maintenance man led me through the rabbit warren of passages.

We walked for more than five minutes before he announced, 'Here you go.'

The door had her name on the outside and the door to its right displayed the name of the person I was really here for - Shaun Metcalf. My heart thudded in my chest.

My escort didn't hang around to see if I needed anything else, he was fifty yards away when I looked his way and turned a corner the very next second, vanishing from sight in the vastness of the crew accommodation area.

I stared at Shaun's door. I was going to have to knock on it.

What did I do then though? Grapple with him and tie him up?

I took some self-defence classes a few years back when Maggie talked me into it. She liked the hunky instructor but after a brief fling she moved on and quit the class just when I was getting into it. How much of it did I remember now? Not much was the likely answer.

You're heavier now, a little voice reminded me helpfully. That should count for something. Was I really going to grab him when he answered the door and accuse him of murder? If he were guilty of two murders already, what would stop him making me his third victim?

Just then Barbie's door opened, her surprised face at seeing me matched mine.

'Hi, Barbie,' I managed.

'Um, hi, Patty. I thought they had you locked up in your suite.'

'They did. Listen, I need to speak with Shaun, will you stay with me for a minute?'

'I need to speak to him too. That's why I came out actually. It sounds like he is wrestling someone in there.'

I looked from her face to his door. Wrestling? As my worry started to rise, I hammered on the door and pressed my ear against the cold steel. I got no answer, so hammered again.

The sound of someone approaching the door from inside preceded it opening. However, the person framed in the doorway wasn't Shaun Metcalf.

It was one of the surly guards from outside my door!

He recognised me too, his eyes widening and his mouth opening to shout.

I kicked him in the nuts as hard as I could.

A grunt of expletive escaped his mouth as the air rushed from his body. He called me something unpleasant and crumpled to his knees. I was shocked at myself. I hadn't kicked a boy in the groin since Billy Mascall pulled my ponytail in sixth grade.

'Wow, Patty!' Beside me, Barbie gasped her surprise and then gasped again when I grabbed her elbow to drag her over the now prone guard and into Shaun's cabin.

I put a finger to my lips so Barbie might understand the need for quiet. We could both hear someone moving about deeper into the cabin.

'Dean get back here and finish the job with me, will you?' The man's voice came from a door at the back of the cabin that I took to be the bathroom. What on earth had I stumbled upon now?

'That's not Shaun's voice,' Barbie whispered.

I glanced about, looking for a weapon. When nothing presented itself, I picked up a discarded dinner plate and advanced on the door the voice came from. Crumbs spilled on the deck unnoticed, my pulse banging in my head yet again.

'Grab his legs,' the voice demanded just as we drew level and could see inside. There was a man on the deck and another man crouched over him. I couldn't see the face of the man on the deck, but I was certain it had to be Shaun. The man crouching over him was another one of the guards from Schooner's pack.

When he got no response to his request, the guard looked up. Just in time to catch the dinner plate in his face as I swung it. The plate broke, but my hope that he would magically fall down unconscious was to be denied as he rose to his feet, blood coming from a cut across the bridge of his nose.

He said a bad word as he came at me, arms rising to grab my face.

I squealed in fright, backing speedily away from the menace to my front. I bumped into Barbie who wasn't moving and found myself stuck.

I couldn't see her, but Barbie was fiddling with her pockets and not paying attention to what was happening to her front.

The guard was on his feet, rage filling his eyes as he lunged for me.

How much of my self-defence training did I remember? I could see that he was going to grab me with his right hand, so since I didn't have time to shove Barbie out of the way, what I needed to do was turn into him and grab his wrist before he got to me. I could parry his other arm and elbow him hard in the face as I stomped on his instep and maybe knee him in the groin.

Yeah, I could make this work! I could tell by his face he wasn't expecting any resistance and that gave me an advantage.

I spun off my left foot to grab his right wrist, his face showing surprise as I moved toward him suddenly instead of flinching away. Then I swung my other arm around in a wide arc to block any attempt to grab me with his left hand and that was where I realised that I didn't remember any of my self-defence training.

I could do it in my head, but in practice I was lost. Instead of disabling the man, my move just spun me into him with the result that we were then spooning standing up.

The significantly larger, stronger, and heavier man swept a leg out to knock me off my feet, then followed me to the deck where he instantly had me pinned.

Knowing I was caught, I fought back anyway, kicking, flailing, and struggling for all I was worth because I knew Commander Schooner was sure to lock me in a cage this time. Above me, Barbie yelled something and suddenly the man's weight was gone as he threw himself backward to get away.

'Arrrgh! Arrrgh, my eyes!' he screamed while flailing at his face.

Barbie had sprayed him with mace!

I rolled onto my front, taking Barbie's hand as she helped me up.

'I keep this in case boys ever get too amorous,' she revealed, smiling through the fear etched on her face.

By our feet, the fallen Shaun Metcalf was coming around. He had blood on his face from a cut inside his hairline.

I yelled, 'Quick, grab an arm.'

Instinctively, Barbie did as I asked, and we dragged him out of the bathroom. With Shaun on his feet, we turned to find our path blocked. Between us and the door was Dean the guard, just getting up and at least partially recovered from the injury I gave him.

Between laboured breaths, he wheezed, 'I'm gonna kill you.' He was coming in my direction, clearly not able to stand fully upright, but determined to do his job anyway.

He didn't get far. No more than a few steps when Barbie maced him as well. Just like his partner, he went down clutching his face and screaming.

'That's for not being very nice,' said Barbie as she delicately tucked the mace back in the pocket of her stretchy pants.

Holding his head and wincing, Shaun asked, 'Who are you?'

It was Barbie who answered. 'I'm Barbie, I live next door.'

'That's nice,' he replied, clearly not certain that it was. 'Now what the heck is going on?'

'We need to move,' I said rather than answer his question. 'Your friends won't be down forever.' We had to step over Dean on our way out, his attempt to trip us and block our exit rewarded with another kick to the nether region which ended his efforts instantly.

'Remind me not to annoy you,' murmured Shaun. 'Do either of you know who they are?'

'You mean you don't know?' I stared at Shaun, unsure what to make of the shift in my plan. Somehow, I found myself protecting the man I came to accuse of murder. The man I thought guilty of killing Jack Langley was being targeted by the same men who were keeping me locked in my suite. What did that mean?

'Barbie, we need to get somewhere safe. Is there a room we can go to where we won't be disturbed for a few minutes?'

'Girls' restroom?' she suggested. I nodded and two fast corners later she shoved open a door to her left and we all spilled through it.

I leaned against the door for a second, letting my heartrate drop from *dangerously high* to the less scary *probably going to have a heart attack*.

'What's going on, Patty?' Barbie asked as we found ourselves tucked out of the way and able to gather our thoughts.

The main thought in my head was that we were trapped if they caught us in here. The guards hadn't made it out of Shaun's room before we escaped the passage his cabin was in so I was hoping, once again, that they had entirely too much ship to search.

I turned to Shaun Metcalf. 'Did you kill Jack Langley?'

He stared right at me, his furrowed brow trying to work out what I had just said. 'Jack Langley?' he replied slowly. 'What do you know about Jack Langley?'

I returned his gaze. Shaun looked genuinely mystified by my question, so I did my best to fill in a few blanks. 'I know that the two of you stole a precious gem many years ago and he escaped while you went to jail.'

'Escaped with the damned jewel and abandoned me,' he snapped out to correct me.

I continued anyway, 'I know you lost your fingers that night and that was how they caught you. And I know Jack was murdered in his cabin three days ago. How much coincidence are you willing to believe, Shaun?' I was struggling to believe that he wasn't involved but sadly, I had to admit that his dumbfounded act, if it was one, was convincing. When I combined that with what looked like two of Commander Schooner's guards trying to kill him, I had to admit that, yet again, I had no idea what was going on.

Shaun looked right at me when he said, 'You're telling me that Jack Langley was on this ship and someone murdered him?'

I didn't answer him, I had another question, 'If it wasn't you, then who else would want him dead?'

Shaun blew out an exasperated breath, 'Maybe everyone? The man was a parasite. He stole from everyone and no one ever suspected him because he was so suave and charming.' I couldn't disagree. Shaun sagged against the counter behind him. 'I can't believe he was on this ship. God, I hated that man. I probably would have killed him myself if I had known.'

I believed what he was saying but I wasn't finished with the questions, 'What did the security guards want with you?'

166

As he opened his mouth to answer, a beeping noise came from a speaker mounted in the ceiling, then Commander Schooner's South African accent came over the address system, 'This is a message to all crew. Be on the lookout for a passenger in the crew accommodation area. The passenger's name is Patricia Fisher. She is to be considered extremely dangerous. Last seen wearing pink flannel pyjamas, she may be accompanied by two accomplices, Barbara Berkeley, and Shaun Metcalf. Security have been dispatched to apprehend all three. However, if you see her, or her accomplices, you are tasked, as a member of this ship's crew, to detain them. Good luck.'

'Oh, my God,' whispered Barbie, utter terror making her voice almost silent. Dean and the other guard must have recovered enough to trigger the alarm.

'Shaun,' I snapped. 'What did the guards want with you?'

He looked as bewildered as Barbie. 'I don't know. They were in my cabin when I got there. They grabbed me and knocked me out. One of them whacked me over the head. When I woke up, you were there. Now how about you answer a question for me? I am going to assume from that announcement that you are Patricia Fisher. Why don't you tell me why they want you and what it is that I am suddenly an accomplice to?'

'They think I killed Jack Langley. I've been trying to find out who did kill him for the last three days. I thought it had to be you. Your presence on the boat is just too much ...' I stopped speaking mid-sentence as something occurred to me, then asked a different question. 'How is it that you came to be on board?'

'I was recruited,' he replied with an innocent shrug.

That just led to more questions, but the restroom door opened, the young woman framed in the doorway now frozen as she took in the three of us all looking at her.

She held up her hands. 'I don't want any trouble,' she said as she backed out of the room, but as the door swung shut again, we could hear her yelling outside. 'They're here! Someone help me! They're here. I found them!'

Cursing my luck for the hundredth time in the last hour, I yanked the door open, yelling, 'Come on!' to Barbie and Shaun as they were both too stunned to have started moving.

The next second we were running along the passageway in the opposite direction to the woman who was still yelling for help. Her efforts worked too.

As we turned the next corner, I saw more security guards in their pristine white uniforms running along the passageway toward us. They were a hundred yards away but moving much faster than I could manage and Shaun was slower even than me.

Where were we going anyway? It wasn't like we could escape the ship. In the lead, Barbie jinked to her left, taking a new passageway that ran perpendicular to the one we were leaving. I was getting out of breath and slowing down, but just as I was thinking our situation was hopeless, Jermaine appeared from a doorway just ahead of us.

We skidded to a halt. Was he still mad at me? Was he here to regain his name by capturing us himself?

'Quick,' he beckoned as we were just staring at him and not moving, 'there're stairs this way.'

Barbie, being naturally faster since she looked like a gazelle in human form, bounded up the stairs three at a time. Shaun was no fitter than I and stank of cigarettes which explained his wheezing for breath after only a fifty-yard dash. I pushed Shaun after Barbie while Jermaine closed the door.

My butler caught up with me easily on the stairs. 'I came as soon as I heard the announcement. Isn't that the other jewel thief?'

'Hi, Shaun Metcalf, very confused steward,' wheezed Shaun.

'I'm sorry, Jermaine, I don't know what's happening,' I admitted. 'Two of Schooner's security guards were attacking Shaun when I got to his cabin.'

'Attacking him?' Jermaine's voice betrayed the same disbelief I held. The attack wasn't imagined though.

'We need to get to a public place!' I yelled. I had no breath for anything else. I wanted to find the captain and force him to listen to reason. I was innocent and members of the ship's security detachment had just tried to hurt the one man I thought might be the killer. Okay, he wasn't the first man I thought might be the killer, but despite my incompetence as an amateur sleuth, there was something screwy going on and we were getting closer to finding out what it was.

As we raced up the stairs, the door below us slammed open and the guards started up the stairs behind us. They were three flights behind, but they were going to catch Shaun and me in no time.

On the next landing, we caught up to Barbie who appeared to have stopped so we could catch up.

'This is silly,' Barbie expressed with a frown. She wasn't even slightly out of breath but looked disinclined to keep running. 'Why don't we just explain that we haven't done anything and let them escort us to Commander Schooner. I'm sure we can sort it all out.'

A deafening boom echoed in the stairwell and a hole appeared in the steel bulkhead by Shaun's face.

They were shooting at us!

I glanced over the handrail. Both men had weapons in their hands and were running up the stairs again. They saw me look down and cracked out two more shots.

I screamed, 'That's why!' as I tried to maintain control of my bladder.

The stairs wound around and around with an intermediate landing between each deck. Screaming as we went, the four of us ran up the next flight and burst through the first door we came to. We were on the thirteenth deck, three decks beneath the first sun deck.

'We have to jam this door!' yelled Shaun. He was barely able to breathe, but he could still think, and he had a plan. The sound of glass shattering turned out to be the former jewel thief rescuing a fire axe. While I stared in wonder, questioning the effectiveness of an axe in a gun fight, he threaded it neatly between the fire door handles, checked it secured them and sagged against the wall.

Seconds later the security guards hit the outside of the doors, rattling them in their frame but the axe handle held. Two more booms rang out and two dents appeared in the steel doors as the bullets deformed the metal. They couldn't penetrate it though.

We were safe, perhaps only briefly, but a sigh of relief escaped my lips, nevertheless.

'Would one of you now tell me what is going on?' Shaun pleaded. He was leaning against the wall, still trying to catch his breath.

I said, 'We need to keep moving before they radio to their colleagues and arrange a team to head us off. We can walk and talk, right?' Jermaine slipped an arm around Shaun's shoulders to get him moving. I turned to Barbie. 'Can you find us a way out of here? We need to get to the captain or at least somewhere public so they can't shoot us.'

'Where are all the people?' wailed Barbie as she darted ahead to find a way out. 'There're like ten thousand people on this ship, how come we are alone? Where are we even?'

'I don't know,' answered Jermaine. 'Wherever we are, I have never been here before.'

Ahead of us, Barbie was trying doors. Most of them were locked and those that weren't led to maintenance rooms or storerooms. They might be good to hide in but hiding wasn't a strategy that could have any long-term success.

I remembered a question I thought of earlier but hadn't had the chance to ask, 'Shaun, tell me again how you came to be on the ship.'

'I was recruited right out of jail. I was coming up for parole and they had a job waiting for me. I didn't have to take it, but if I hadn't, they probably wouldn't have let me out.'

'That's it? You don't know where the job offer came from?'

'Nope. Well, not at the time. There was a pair of men in the parole hearing that were there to guarantee my employment. Normally, ex-cons

171

are not allowed to travel for a period after release but someone had made some kind of assurance that went with the job, so I got out and they brought me straight to the boat. I didn't see them again until they turned up in my cabin and tried to kill me earlier.'

'What? The two guards are the ones that collected you from jail?' It was astonishing news but provided another big fat clue.

He nodded, 'Yup. I probably should have known there was something devious going on, but I just wanted out of jail. I didn't really care why I had been offered the job and, if I'm being honest about it, I didn't ask. I was stealing things before I could walk. I was always a criminal. This is the first real job I have ever had, and I like it. I wish I'd never met Jack Langley. My life could have turned out completely different.'

'How so?' I asked.

'I met him when I was a kid,' Shaun continued his story. 'He was a couple of years older than me and he took me under his wing. I thought it was a good thing at the time because he had big plans about getting rich. But by the time I was fifteen, I had been in juvie hall four times. We just kept getting caught. It didn't put him off though, he said we were learning our craft and getting better so that one day we could pull off the one big job that would change our lives.'

'When he got busted again, he went to the state penitentiary because he had turned eighteen and already had a juvenile record. I didn't see him for twenty years after that. Then one day he turns up babbling on about this huge sapphire they have on display at the New York Geological Society. We stole it, but I slipped and fell on the way out and my hand got impaled. Jack could have helped me get free, but he abandoned me and took the sapphire. I had to yank my hand free before the cops turned up which is how I lost my fingers. A couple of days later I got busted in hospital anyway. I never saw Jack again and they threw the book at me.'

'How come you didn't rat him out to get your sentence reduced? I asked.

'Because the word rat is exactly what I would have been. It goes against the code. I would never have made it out of jail alive.' His smile was rueful.

'I found stairs,' Barbie called from fifty feet in front of us. She was holding open a door and indicating with her head.

As we scurried through the door and started up the stairs, I started to feel hopeful. We hadn't been chased for several minutes and hadn't seen anyone in that time. It was almost as if we were out for a peaceful stroll.

Four levels up, the sign on the door announced we had reached the Lido deck.

'Is this one of the public areas?' I asked.

'Very public, madam' replied Jermaine. 'There will be passengers and crew when we get outside, but I can't tell from here whether this will open onto one of the open deck areas or into one of the shopping and eating areas.'

I bit my lip. 'Let's find out.'

Through the door was a short passageway to another door, but the next door had a round porthole style window in it through which light was coming. It wasn't daylight from outside though, or at least not directly. The door opened into a shopping area, the same one I had been in just an hour or so ago with the Italian village square in it. We stepped tentatively out and began walking across the open area.

'That address system message,' I started, 'would that have gone out to all areas of the ship?'

Jermaine shook his head. 'Goodness, no, madam. That went only to the crew area. Why?'

'Because we are being watched.'

Confrontation

I had to admit that I might have stared as well. We were an eclectic group; a butler in full gear with tails, a gym-bunny in Lycra, a middle-aged woman in her pyjamas and a grey-haired older man in a steward's uniform with blood on his face.

We were making a beeline for the escalators to go up another level, but two sets of eyes at a table by the fountain were tracking us and they were not the only ones looking our way. They were the only ones that stood up though, instantly revealing themselves as two more of Schooner's security guards.

Undoubtedly placed in an open space in case we appeared, they were on their feet and moving. Their route would intercept ours before we got to the escalators.

I shouted, 'Run!' and pushed Shaun ahead of me to get him moving.

The guards had to weave between tables before they could start running. It gave us the few extra seconds we needed to get to the escalator first. For good measure, I hooked a chair as I ran and threw it across the deck toward them as they cleared the last table and got into the open.

All around us people were watching the entertainment. The patrons eating their brunch were standing up to get a better view. The chair zipped across the tiled deck, but the first guard just put a leg out to stop it and casually spoke into a radio on his lapel.

I didn't like that he wasn't chasing us, not that I wanted to be chased, but I took his relaxed attitude to be a sign of something worse. When the escalator neared the top, I saw what the worse thing was.

Two more guards were on the next level waiting for us. I was the last one on, so had Shaun, Jermaine, and Barbie ahead of me. At the front, Barbie was trying to back up even as the escalator was pushing her forward. One of the guards silently beckoned for her to come to him, his face an ugly sneer as if he were looking forward to handling her.

I glanced behind me to see the guards from below step onto the escalator. They were following us up to join their colleagues on the next deck.

We were effectively trapped.

Inevitably, the escalator spilled Barbie onto the deck, the rest of us right on her heels. The nearest guard, the one who had been beckoning to her, whipped out an arm to grab her around her left wrist and yanked her forward out of the way so his colleague could get to the rest of us.

As he did so, he sneered, 'Come on, babe, it's time go to.'

Then his colleague reached for Jermaine as he came off the escalator behind Barbie.

He displayed a broad grin when he said, 'You too, Homo.'

I couldn't see Jermaine's face, but the homophobic insult flicked a switch somewhere deep inside him because the next thing I knew, the guard was upside down on the deck with Jermaine's foot on his head.

Jermaine had grasped the man's outstretched hand as it reached for him, pushed it one way just enough for the man to react and try to pull free, then reversed momentum and lunged in the direction the man was going, which forced the guard's centre of balance to extend past his feet. As he toppled, Jermaine whipped out a long leg that arced high and over the man's shoulder to follow him down. In two seconds, the dominant position the guards felt they had was reversed.

Oblivious to events, the escalator kept on rolling forward, pushing Shaun and then me onto the deck where the other guard had now let go of Barbie's arm and was swinging a clubbing fist at Jermaine.

Jermaine simply ducked it and as the man's momentum carried him onward, Jermaine flicked out a leg to deliver a hard kick to the guard's lower back. Barbie, Shaun, and I all stared at Jermaine with our mouths open.

'Don't just gawp, madam,' he instructed. 'Run!'

So, run we did. Straight through the nearest door with the two guards from the deck below chasing after us. The door led to a supply area and had to be buzzed open using a chip card. I had three different members of crew with me though, so with the guards hot on our heels, we all tumbled inside, pushed the doors shut and threw the two deadbolts to stop the guards following us.

I leaned against the door, trying to catch my breath again, then jumped out of my skin as the guard's face appeared right next to mine. The door had porthole style windows in it, and he was mouthing obscenities and threats through it. Thankfully, I couldn't really hear him.

I pushed away from the door on wobbly legs.

'Where are we?' I asked. Without needing to herd them, our oddly mixed group were already moving down the corridor away from the door.

'Never mind that,' said Barbie, staring at Jermaine. 'When did you become a ninja?'

'Yeah,' I echoed.

Jermaine shrugged, 'It was one of the requirements for the butler job. In order to care for royalty, should they decide to cruise with us, the butler must be able to double as their personal guard. I started martial arts classes when I was four years old and ... well, I guess I got good. Just because I am gay, doesn't mean I cannot fight.'

None of us had a response to that, but noise coming from the doors we had locked made us hurry as it was clear the guards were trying to force their way through.

'Can they get through?' asked Shaun.

'Let's not hang around to find out, eh?' I replied. 'Jermaine, what's the quickest way to the bridge?'

He led us through another door, saying, 'We need to get to the central elevator bank. We can ride it all the way to the top deck.'

'The bridge is above the top deck,' I pointed out.

'That's as close as we can get, I'm afraid. All I can do is get us there and hope the guards agree to let us pass.'

'Why don't we just call the captain?' Barbie asked.

There was a moment's pause during which Jermaine stared at Barbie as if she was being the stereotypical dumb blonde he knew she wasn't. Then, as I watched, Jermaine's expression clouded, and he slapped his forehead. I gave him a quizzical look. 'There's a crew intercom,' he explained. 'Even without a radio, we can still get through to the bridge.'

'Oh, my God.' We had been running and getting chased and shot at and generally threatened for the last half hour and we could have just used an intercom to speak with the captain all along. 'Where's the nearest intercom?'

'I'm not sure,' he admitted, 'But there will be one next to the elevator.'

Beside me, Shaun was still wheezing from the effort of our escape but levered himself upright now. 'There's one closer.'

With that he set off, leading the way for the first time. He was right though, leading us around a couple of corners, we came out into an open area where several passages joined and there, on the wall, was a handset on a cable set next to a speaker.

'Here goes nothing,' said Jermaine as he lifted the handset and pressed a button.

Moments later a voice could be heard faintly at the other end. Jermaine asked to be connected to the bridge and after another few seconds a different voice came on the line.

'Bridge.' The single word was all Jermaine got as a prompt to start speaking.

'This is Special Rating Clarke, I'm the butler in the Windsor Suite. I need to speak with the captain.' There was a pause before he spoke again, this time in urgent terms. 'No, not Commander Schooner. It has to be the captain and Commander Schooner cannot know I am calling.' Another pause as the other person asked questions. 'Why? I cannot tell you that.' A pause. 'Because it is sensitive.'

Jermaine slumped with relief as the captain finally came on the line almost a minute later. Once again, we got to hear only Jermaine's side of the conversation.

'Yes, sir. I know, sir. This is an emergency, sir.'

To me it sounded like he was losing the conversation while getting a good dressing down for disturbing the one man that might be able to help

179

me. I put one hand on Jermaine's chest and held out the other for him to give me the phone handset.

'Let me try,' I requested in an insistent tone. As he handed it over, I started speaking, 'Captain, this is Mrs Fisher, the guest in the Windsor Suite.'

'Mrs Fisher?' the captain stammered. He was not expecting to hear my voice and it caught him off guard. 'The intercom says you are calling from a storeroom on the sixteenth deck. Surely, you are confined to your suite?'

I ignored the question. 'Captain Huntley I have been wanting to talk to you since my incarceration and Commander Schooner has been blocking my attempts to do so.'

'Why do you want to talk to me, Mrs Fisher?'

'Because I am innocent of the crimes I have been accused of.'

'Commander Schooner assures me that is not the case. I'm afraid you will have to explain your case to the authorities on St Kitts, Mrs Fisher. We are simply not equipped to....'

I cut him off, 'Commander Schooner is the murderer.'

'What?' Captain Huntley spluttered. 'That's preposterous! I've known Robert Schooner personally for more than a decade. He ...'

I cut him off again. 'I have evidence that cannot be disputed. If you can offer me safe passage, I will bring it to you.'

There was a confused pause as the captain tried to process my claims.

'Why would you need safe passage? What are you doing in a sixteenth deck storeroom anyway?'

'Hiding from Commander Schooner's goons. They have been shooting at us.'

'What?' he spluttered again. 'Mrs Fisher, I cannot believe what you are telling me. What is really happening?'

Jermaine, who was crowding the handset to hear the conversation, spoke again, 'It's all true, sir. We are coming to you now, but we are being chased.'

Just then, a crashing noise and the sound of boots thumping on the deck told us the guards had found a way through the locked doors.

'Quick,' squeaked Barbie, 'through here.'

'We have to go!' I shouted into the intercom. 'Schooner is behind it all!' I wanted to hear him confirm he was sending someone to help us, but there was no time to wait.

Schooner's guards were coming, and they were coming for us.

Barbie held open a door for everyone to dart through and once again we were running, the voices of the guards not far behind us as someone yelled instructions into a radio.

Jermaine darted ahead, his long legs carrying him faster than even Barbie could go. At the end of the narrow passageway, he grabbed the door. 'The elevator is right here,' he called, beckoning urgently for us to hurry.

I was winded and poor old Shaun looked about ready to expire from lack of oxygen. Jermaine was right though, as we got through the door, a pair of silver elevator doors shone tantalisingly before us in a square area that had four passages leading off from it.

'Arrrgh!' screamed Barbie and for good reason. Through the glass porthole window set into each door, we could see guards running along each of the four passages toward us. There was nowhere left to go.

Jermaine's index finger jabbed the elevator call button with desperation, but in the storage area the elevators were not fitted with a display to show which deck the cars were on. We could hear them moving but had no way of knowing when they might arrive.

I could see guns in the guards' hands, their sidearms drawn and ready for use. Idly, I wondered if they would just shoot us all and claim we tried to fight our way out after planting weapons on us. It seemed like something they could get away with.

They were yards away now, we had seconds until they burst through the doors.

Then the elevator pinged.

As one, the four of us spun to get in, but stopped dead as yet more guards looked out at us, their own weapons drawn.

My heart stopped beating. Now there truly was nowhere left to go, and not the slightest chance of escape.

'Good morning, Mrs Fisher,' said the captain as he stepped calmly from the elevator into the small room. I hadn't seen him standing between all the other white uniforms.

Almost simultaneously, the four doors leading into our small room from the adjoining passages burst open as armed guards flooded in. They were shouting instructions for us to, 'Get on the floor,' and, 'Hands behind your backs.' Everyone was pointing weapons at everyone else and most of the guards just looked confused because they thought they were all on the same team.

The captain's voice cut across everyone else, 'Desist!' His voice, the commanding tone it carried, instantly caused all of his guards to pause while they listened for his next command, 'Now then, gentlemen. Please lower your weapons.'

The smart guards in their pristine white uniforms all did as requested, with two exceptions: the two guards that we had interrupted in Shaun's cabin. They were easy to recognise because their eyes were still streaming and red from the mace attack.

'They're dangerous, sir,' said the first, his weapon pointing at Shaun's centre of mass.

'Yeah,' agreed his companion, 'she killed Mr Langley and Lieutenant Davis and then she attacked us in Metcalf's cabin. They're in it together.'

The captain turned his attention to me.

'Is that true, Mrs Fisher?' Then remembering that I still had a gun pointing at me, he turned back to the guards. 'Lower your weapons, gentlemen, or I shall have you disarmed.'

There was no disputing the calm insistence in his voice. The two men looked at each other, each tussling internally to decide what they should do. If they were wondering whether they could shoot us and get away with it, they decided they could not. Reluctantly and slowly, they placed their sidearms back into their holsters.

'Mrs Fisher?' the captain prompted.

'As I assured you a few minutes ago, I have had nothing to do with any of the thefts and deaths, except that I unwittingly became the subject of a plot to cover up the theft of a priceless jewel from the man who originally stole it.'

The captain raised an eyebrow. 'Go on.'

'Perhaps we could go somewhere else for this?' I suggested. 'It's been quite the morning between all the fighting, chasing and being shot at. I really wouldn't mind something to drink.'

'Patty!' chided Barbie, ever conscious of my diet.

'Water will be fine,' I added.

The Big Reveal

There were far too many of us to make travelling anywhere in the elevators a tenable solution, so, led by the captain and trailed by a small platoon of white-uniformed guards, we made our way back through the passages that connected the storage area to the passenger area of the ship.

The captain issued instructions as he walked. 'Lieutenant Baker, send for Commander Schooner,' he instructed one guard, who dashed away to find the ship's number two man. He also detailed men off to secure Shaun's cabin and Barbie's for good measure and sent another pair of men to arrange refreshments to be taken to briefing room seven.

I had no idea where or what briefing room seven was, but I soon found out as it was located on the deck we were already on. After emerging back into the passenger area via a different door to the one we fled down just a few minutes ago, we crossed a wide expanse of deck, went through another door and into a large room. It was laid out for someone at the front to give instructions to people assembled in the rest of the space. A large projector hanging from the ceiling was aimed at a pull-down screen on one wall and next to it was a map of the world laid flat.

'Now then,' said the captain as he poured me a glass of ice water and offered me a seat. 'Please tell me what has been going on, Mrs Fisher,' his tone was encouraging, wanting me to feel relaxed and to believe that he was prepared to listen.

As I opened my mouth to speak, the doors to the briefing room slammed back against their stops and the dreaded Commander Schooner arrived.

He immediately tried to take over.

185

'Ah, well done, sir,' he addressed the captain while shooting me a hateful stare. 'I see you caught her. No need for any further involvement on your part, sir. I'll take it from here. Terribly embarrassing that she gave my guards the slip, of course. You can expect a full report once I have investigated their failing.'

The captain allowed Commander Schooner to shake his hand but did not depart when advised he could do so. It was clearly what Schooner wanted - to isolate me again.

'Actually, Robert,' Captain Huntley addressed the deputy captain by his first name, 'Mrs Fisher had some interesting things to say about your involvement in this affair. Something about a priceless jewel. Perhaps you would like to hear it.'

Commander Schooner cracked a smile as if the captain had just told a joke. Then, he started issuing commands, 'Sorry, sir. You seem to have been taken in by Mrs Fisher's lies. You, you, and you, weapons on them now,' he barked as he jabbed his finger at the three guards nearest to him.

They reacted instantly but as their weapons left their holsters, they then looked confused. Whose orders should they obey?

'Lower your weapons,' ordered the captain, his annoyance at his deputy's attitude beginning to show.

'No, captain.' Commander Schooner moved to bring his greater height to bear against his superior. 'Several of my guards have been assaulted. Two report that Miss Berkeley used chemical spray on them. Her butler was expressly forbidden from aiding her and yet here he is, and I see that you have also caught her main accomplice, the former partner in crime of Jack Langley, Shaun Metcalf, who took a job on the ship to exact revenge on the man that left him to rot in jail.'

186

He turned to face me though he continued to address the captain, 'I have been trying to protect you from the terrible events that have been going on since Mrs Fisher came aboard, but clearly it is time I explained.' He turned back to the captain as he continued to embellish his lie.

'Sir, you are already aware that Mrs Fisher was seen leaving the upper deck restaurant with Mr Langley the night that he was murdered. She was subsequently found in his cabin attempting to recover her purse which she left there when committing the crime. She concocted a story about finding her rings missing to explain her presence in his room and a search of her suite did not reveal them. At first, I assumed she had simply hidden them in her safe since she refused to reveal the whereabouts of the key, but today they were found in the cabin of one of our stewards, Shaun Metcalf, a former criminal partner of Mr Langley. My investigation led me to believe Jack Langley was the person responsible for the recent spate of jewel thefts - the thefts coincide with his time on board.'

'I learned much of this through my work with Flint Magnum who was hired by the Queen of Sweden after Jack Langley stole priceless diamonds from her. It would seem though, that there were other priceless items in his possession. Through her butler, Mrs Fisher was able to learn today that we were now aware of Mr Metcalf's past and went to retrieve them before they could be discovered. I believe that further investigation will reveal that Mrs Fisher is known to Shaun Metcalf and the two of them cooked up a plot to kill Jack Langley so that they could recover the items in his possession and to exact revenge through his murder.'

I had to admit that I was impressed by his ability to concoct a lie. His performance was convincing. Most of my brain wanted me to scream in his face that his words were nothing but lies, yet I managed to find an inner calm where the more rational parts of me chose to listen instead.

He was lying. But hidden in his lies were truths I needed to hear.

'Mrs Fisher murdered Lieutenant Davis when she needed to escape her suite and liaise with her accomplice. I believe Miss Berkeley became involved at this point and used her looks to lure Lieutenant Davis inside the suite where Mrs Fisher murdered him. The motive for Miss Berkeley's involvement being nothing other than the offer of riches. Mrs Fisher is, as one can tell by her clothes, not a lady of wealth and could never afford the suite she is staying in. The royal suite was part of her ruse. She played the role of a rich widow on an around the world trip to attract Mr Langley. Her plan to have him invite her into his suite so she could murder him and steal whatever jewels he had played out perfectly in less than twenty-four hours from coming on board. You can see her rings have recently been removed and my research revealed that she is, in fact, still married.'

The captain raised an eyebrow in my direction but refrained from speaking.

Commander Schooner continued lying, 'Mrs Fisher intended to commit her crime, then cancel her trip and get her money back. You are aware, sir, that she has made an attempt to book a flight home, yes?'

Looking at me, the captain nodded, 'Yes, I was aware.'

'Her mistake was in leaving her purse in Jack Langley's suite. Had she not done so and then been caught attempting to retrieve it, we might never have identified her as the killer. All that has come since - the involvement of Miss Berkeley, the death of Lieutenant Davis, and the attack on Flint Magnum, have all occurred because I was not swift enough to realise how dangerous she was and how devious. For that, I apologise.'

'What happened to Flint Magnum?' I asked.

'Feigning ignorance, Mrs Fisher?' scoffed Commander Schooner. 'I accept that it probably wasn't you that bashed in his skull, but it will have occurred on your orders. No doubt, sir, she planned to hide with the

188

jewels and escape the ship somehow once we reached St Kitts. Flint Magnum's career and reputation depended on recovering the missing jewels. My guess is that he either confronted Mrs Fisher after she escaped her suite, or she actively sought him out to remove another threat from the playing board.'

My mind swirled from the news that Flint had been attacked. Commander Schooner, or his thugs, had been trying to clean house, getting rid of anyone that knew about the sapphire which included Flint Magnum, Shaun Metcalf, and of course me, Jermaine, and Barbie. They got to Flint and were interrupted in the act of dealing with Shaun.

Commander Schooner finally fell silent, and no one spoke for several seconds while the captain, clearly deep in thought, paced the room and tapped a finger to his lips. When he finally looked up, he said, 'Well done, Commander Schooner.'

'No!' I wailed. I couldn't believe the captain had been convinced by his lies, but then I had to concede the circumstantial evidence, such as trying to get a flight home, was quite damning.

The captain wasn't finished though. 'I think perhaps I would like to hear from Mrs Fisher now.' All eyes swung to look at me. I was staring at Commander Schooner - there was rage in his eyes, but he remained mute. 'Mrs Fisher,' the captain prompted.

'Okay,' I started, trying to gather my thoughts so I could explain my theory in a way that would make sense. 'This goes back almost four decades to when two young men embarked on a life of crime. They broke into people's houses and stole from them. One of the men, Jack Langley, liked to steal jewels and had his mind on pulling off the kind of job that would let him retire. Both men spent time in and out of jail and through their incarceration, lost contact. That is until one day Jack Langley

189

reappeared at his old accomplice's place with a plan to steal a fat, priceless sapphire.'

I held my breath for a moment and twisted on the spot to lock eyes with as many people as possible. I wanted to connect with them and to be sure they were paying attention.

'The Sapphire of Zangrabar, so called because it was given as a gift from the Maharaja to his wife, is a jewel so famous that once they pulled it off, Jack discovered he couldn't sell it. During the robbery, his partner had an accident and lost two of his fingers.' I turned and pointed to Shaun, who raised his damaged hand helpfully so all could see. The captain was good enough to look surprised. 'Leaving his fingers at the scene ensured he went to jail for the theft, but he never revealed the name of his partner who fled with the jewel and left him to rot in prison. Shaun Metcalf was finally released after thirty years and deliberately recruited to work on this ship.'

I took a sip of water, doing my best to keep my hand steady when I lifted the glass to my lips.

'In the meantime, Jack Langley, suspected of many crimes in many countries, but rich enough to afford a suite aboard this ship, lived a life of luxury spending his ill-gotten gains. He perpetuated his lifestyle by continuing to steal from rich widows and lonely wives who were dumb enough or desperate enough to fall for his charms. He tried the same trick on me but drew a blank because I have no jewellery worth stealing. He took my wedding rings nevertheless which is how I came to be in his suite the morning he was murdered.'

'Flint Magnum told me his real name is Neil Hammond, but that was a lie also. His real name is Samuel Lawrence.' I locked eyes with Commander Schooner, certain that if my guess was wrong, his face would show it. He didn't react at all, and I pressed on. 'And though it is true that he came aboard several weeks ago to investigate Jack Langley, he wasn't hired by the Queen of Sweden as he claims. In truth he is an insurance recovery agent working for Axiz Insurers, who having paid out when the sapphire was stolen thirty years ago, are still looking to recover the debt.' I was walking as I talked, the other people in the room tracking me with their eyes as they all listened intently. Even Commander Schooner was silent, but I think that was only because I hadn't got to him yet.

'Commander Schooner learned from Samuel Lawrence that he was on board to track down a famous jewel when he attempted to recruit the commander's help. Commander Schooner's position as head of security made him the right man to approach, but he hadn't realised Schooner would use that information for his own gain.'

'Preposterous,' spat the ship's second in command.

I ignored him. 'Shaun Metcalf was recruited after Commander Schooner did his own research into Jack Langley. It wasn't that hard to track down the likely accomplice in prison once he knew the name of the jewel Samuel Lawrence was attempting to recover. Shaun didn't meet the person that offered him the job. He was collected by Schooner's two most loyal … henchmen, is that the right term?' I questioned. 'Can you point to the two men who collected you from prison, Shaun?'

Just across from me, Shaun raised a nervous arm to point at the two men who had been trying to kill him earlier. They both glanced around for an escape route, but there was none to be had.

'Secure their weapons,' instructed the captain and instantly the four guards nearest them drew their firearms while two more took the sidearms from the thugs' holsters. Commander Schooner didn't react at all, his confidence unflappable.

191

I continued my summation, 'I believe that when a check is conducted, the jail discharge paperwork will show Commander Schooner's signature, who having learned there was a thief on board with priceless jewels in his possession, set about a plot to make himself rich. He recruited the two men you have just disarmed, no doubt promising them a cut or a promotion or something …'

'How much of this rubbish do we have to listen to?' asked the deputy captain while feigning boredom.

The captain gave him a level stare, saying, 'All of it, Commander Schooner.'

'The night I came on board, I disturbed Samuel Lawrence's attempt to catch Jack Langley in the act of seducing and robbing a rich widow. I did this by accidentally getting drunk and passing out.' Hardly my finest moment. 'Now possibly Samuel intended to find me in the morning, hoping to discover that I had been robbed in the night and could use that information to force a search of Jack's suite. But I was up early, and Jack was already dead. Commander Schooner killed Jack but when he took Jack's safe key, he found the safe empty.'

Captain Huntley frowned in his confusion. 'Were there no jewels after all?'

'Oh, there were jewels alright. Jack spotted Samuel's blundering attempts to follow and spy on him and grew suspicious. Having dumped me in my cabin, he proceeded to snatch my rings; why break the habit of a lifetime, but then he took my safe key and stashed his stolen jewels, no doubt including the Sapphire of Zangrabar, in my suite.'

I was making most of it up on the spot, adding together the clues and guessing the rest. It made sense though, and I could see the truth ahead of me like a brightly lit path to walk through the dark on either side.

192

'No one would think to look in my safe, and he no doubt intended to continue to seduce me so he could recover them later, maybe then switching ships since he was under suspicion here.'

'If that were true, then where is the key to your safe?' asked Schooner, desperate to make a point.

I shot him a smile and held up an index finger to beg his indulgence. 'I'm getting to it, Commander, please be patient.' His impatience – a sign of nerves, I believed, was making me feel more confident. As I talked my way through the confusion, it became clearer and clearer. 'Commander Schooner only discovered the jewels were not in Jack's safe after he killed him and took his key, but I presented him with a patsy for the murder when he found my purse in Jack's cabin and could reliably claim I must have been there. The rings I claimed Jack had stolen were not there because Commander Schooner or one of his goons had already found them. Using that as an excuse and needing time to work out what had happened to the jewels, Commander Schooner had me confined to my suite. It was only after doing so that he discovered my safe key was missing and realised that Jack must have taken it.'

'Why would he do that?' asked the captain. He was keeping up, but like everyone else in the room, he was utterly confused.

'Because he knew he was being watched and sensed that Samuel Lawrence or Commander Schooner were going to swoop soon. Jack Langley seized his chance when I passed out and stashed the jewels in my safe. I can only assume he took my purse to get my door key and then left it in his own cabin by accident.'

'So, if Jack Langley took your safe key, where is it?' the captain asked, his voice hushed, quite transfixed by my story.

193

I crinkled my face in disgust as I said, 'It was in Jack's body. He swallowed it in haste when Commander Schooner attacked him. That is why his body was mutilated after death. Commander Schooner didn't know I could get out of my suite via my butler's door, but he wanted to check the safe when the ship was mostly empty after docking in Madeira. He must have checked or used the guard to check that I wasn't in the main living area, then snuck in to check the safe. We'll never know if he tried to bribe Lieutenant Davis and couldn't, or always planned to kill him. Perhaps Schooner left him outside but was then disturbed by the curious lieutenant as he retrieved the jewels. Either way, Commander Schooner murdered Lieutenant Davis in my cabin with one of the knives from the kitchen and left the body to be found later. I couldn't have done it you see, because I was ashore in Madeira.'

The captain's face filled with surprise. 'How did you achieve that?'

'I helped her,' admitted Jermaine.

'So, did I,' added Barbie.

I saw how embarrassed they both were to admit the truth but pressed on with my version of events.

'Commander Schooner now had his jewels, including the enormous sapphire, but missed his chance to get them off the ship in Madeira. He sensed that he needed to eliminate some loose ends such as Shaun Metcalf and it was blind luck that Barbie and I interrupted his henchmen attempting to kill Shaun and plant evidence in his room.'

'What evidence?' the captain wanted to know.

I nodded at the question. I had spotted a small bulge in Shaun's back pocket earlier when we were running away but hadn't had time to confirm what it was until now.

I held my breath as I said, 'Can you turn around please, Shaun?'

He obliged and we all stared at his bum. Shaun was craning his head to look over his own shoulder at his left buttock. The lump in his back pocket looked distinctly like three rings. He fished them out when asked, and there were my missing wedding rings.

'Commander Schooner believed he could sow sufficient evidence together to convince everyone that I was guilty of three murders,' I explained. 'I would be incarcerated in St Kitts and either held there or shipped home but in the months of questioning that would follow, I would continually fail to tell them where the jewels were which would give Schooner enough time to sell them. However, he hadn't counted on me being able to escape my suite and save Shaun.'

'That is a wonderful tale, Mrs Fisher,' chuckled Commander Schooner, his features still relaxed. 'You have no real evidence though. It's all circumstantial.'

I met his smile with one of my own and for the first time, I caught a glimpse of nervousness in his eyes.

'You missed something, Commander.' He tilted his head at me in question. 'A few minutes ago, when you were delivering your lie about my involvement with Shaun, you knew all about his past with Jack Langley.'

A cloud of doubt passed over his features for the first time. He recovered quickly. 'I, ah, I must have heard it from Samuel Lawrence,' he stuttered.

'Samuel Lawrence had no idea who Shaun was. Had never heard of him,' I lied having never asked the insurance recovery agent the question. Schooner's eyes were widening in panic. 'Your guards were in Shaun's cabin an hour ago trying to kill him. When questioned, will they say it was all their idea to bump him off? Or will they reveal it was on your orders?'

The two guards glanced at each other, both looking ready to spill the beans now they sensed they were caught.

Abruptly, Commander Schooner grabbed the man nearest to him, shoved him roughly toward the guards and produced a gun of his own. I screamed as he ran for the door. His eyes were locked on mine, and as he ran, his gun was rising. The barrel was only aiming at one person: me.

Frozen to the spot, all I could do was watch as he pulled the trigger.

The captain slammed into me, knocking my breath out as we both hit the deck, his weight on top of mine. I heard him wince in discomfort, but he rolled off me in the next instant, shouting, 'After him,' at his stunned guards.

'Can I help you up, madam?' asked Jermaine as he loomed over me.

I took his offered hand and clambered back to my feet feeling shaken and in need of a lie down.

That's when I spotted blood on the captain's white uniform. He had taken a bullet for me. High on his left arm, a furrow of uniform was missing where the shot grazed his shoulder. It was bleeding convincingly but would not threaten his life. Nevertheless, it had been a heroic thing to do, and he was now ignoring his wound and the pain he must be feeling to direct his men. They were to take Commander Schooner's two henchmen away and search both their cabins and the deputy captain's.

Seconds later, as I was barely recovering my breath, I jumped again as a man in the white guard's uniform burst back into the briefing room.

'He went overboard, sir!' he reported out of breath.

196

'Show me,' said the captain and followed the man from the room. Not wanting to miss anything, I ran after him, my small entourage of Jermaine, Barbie, and a confused Shaun hard on my heels.

If the report were accurate, Commander Schooner burst onto the deck, ran across it brandishing his gun and shouting at passengers until he reached the port railing whereupon he jumped.

All around were startled looking passengers wondering what on earth was going on. At the railing, we stared at a small blob in the water. He was fourteen decks below us, which equated to at least one hundred and fifty feet and now a few hundred yards clear as the ship sailed on and he stroked for a small island at least two miles away.

'Call the coastguard and have him picked up,' instructed the captain. A lieutenant took the order and hurried away to make it happen. Standing by my side at the railing, Captain Alistair Huntley turned to face me.

'Mrs Fisher,' he started and then paused while trying to work out what to say. 'Mrs Fisher, I believe there is no need to question that Robert Schooner is indeed guilty.'

I chewed on my top lip for a moment as I considered what to say in reply.

'He was not working alone,' I pointed out. 'Some of your security team were recruited by him. They were willing to kill me and anyone on Team Patricia.'

'Team Patricia?'

A small laugh escaped me. It was the first time I had found anything amusing since I boarded the ship.

'Yes, sorry. My butler, Jermaine, and Miss Berkeley. They put everything on the line to help me. It felt very much like it was us against the entire ship. Without their help, Commander Schooner would have got away with murder.'

Captain Huntley nodded.

'Yes. It is clear I need to conduct a thorough investigation and root out those who were involved. I shall also have to come up with a suitable reward for the members of *Team Patricia*.' He grinned broadly, sharing the silly name I gave my friends. 'I cannot apologise enough nor thank you sufficiently for what you have had to suffer through and what you have done to reveal the truth.' I couldn't think of anything to say in reply, so I kept quiet. 'You paid for an around the world cruise, did you not?'

That was a question I could answer. 'Yes.'

He nodded, deep in thought. 'Then I shall insist the cruise line waive the cost of the trip and reimburse you in full. I hope you are better able to enjoy the next three months more peacefully.'

His generosity came as a shock, but I had to concede that I deserved it. What I said was, 'Thank you, Captain. However, I intend to get off in St Kitts and return to England. I have some things to work out with my husband.'

He tilted his head in acknowledgement. 'If you change your mind ...'

While I considered the unexpected option to stay on board, another crewman in white uniform arrived.

He addressed the captain, 'Begging your pardon, sir. A message from the doctor. Mr Lawrence is awake.'

The Sapphire

'Would you care to join me, Mrs Fisher?' asked the captain. Seeing my raised quizzical eyebrow, he added, 'I need to speak with Mr Lawrence – I feel a need to clarify his part in what has transpired. First though, I intend to locate the missing jewellery and most especially the fabled sapphire. In truth, I find myself genuinely curious to see just how big it is.'

'Me too,' I admitted.

'And it seems only right that you should, Mrs Fisher.'

He swivelled on his heels to face a new direction and lifted his right arm, the elbow crooked so that I might take it. In front of all the passengers and crew lining the deck, and under the glorious blue Caribbean skies, I will admit my stomach fluttered just a little as I took his arm and let the handsome captain lead me away.

Curious faces tracked our progress across the deck until we stepped back into the superstructure of the ship. I was wearing my pyjamas still. The bottom three inches of the legs were grimy, and my slippers were ruined from the dirt I tracked through in the storage areas. On the arm of the captain in his pristine white uniform, I had to look utterly ridiculous.

Do you know what? I didn't care one little bit.

He led me to an elevator that required a special access code and a key card to open. It was guarded by another member of the security team, a woman this time.

She snapped out a smart salute as her captain approached.

'Lieutenant Bhukari,' Captain Huntley gave her a nod of acknowledgement.

The elevator took us up to the bridge where the captain advised we would find Commander Schooner's private quarters.

The security team were already there, half a dozen of them dismantling his room. I recognised one as he came to report the team's findings. I scoured my brain to recall his name.

'What do you have, Lieutenant Baker?' Captain Huntley supplied the name before I could drag it from the back of my head.

With eyes glistening with excitement, and a grin he was trying to suppress, Lieutenant Baker said, 'It's here, sir.'

Unexpected Bonus

Samuel Lawrence's head was wrapped in a thick bandage where Schooner's goons had tried to crack it open. One eye was swollen shut but he smiled when we walked in.

'I believe you have good news for me, captain. I understand the sapphire has been recovered.' He was sitting up in bed with a pillow supporting his back and a book in his lap.

'That would appear to be the case, Mr Lawrence,' replied the captain. 'It was found in the cabin of my First Officer. You have this lady to thank. Mrs Fisher's tenacity unravelled the mystery and revealed that my own number two was behind the recent murders and indeed the attack on you.'

'I would never have guessed it,' Samuel admitted glumly. 'I believed Commander Schooner was operating with the best interests of justice. I was the fool feeding him all the information he needed to steal the jewel for himself.'

'What will happen to it now?' I asked.

'The sapphire?' Samuel confirmed. 'It belongs to the Maharaja of Zangrabar but was stolen from the New York Geological Society. Axiz Insurance Brokers paid out when it was stolen and not recovered, so technically they own it although I am sure the Maharaja will be willing to pay to get it back from them.'

'As I understand it, Mr Lawrence, there is a substantial reward for its return.'

'That's correct,' Samuel replied cautiously.

'And it was Mrs Fisher who recovered it,' the captain continued, 'so I believe the reward is hers, yes?'

My pulse beat a hard staccato at the news. I had no idea there was any kind of a reward. What exactly did substantial mean?

'Eh, no, I don't think so,' said Samuel sternly.

The captain leaned forward, 'Let me put it this way, Mr Lawrence; either Mrs Fisher gets the reward, or you don't get the sapphire back.'

'Now see here!' snapped Samuel, his temperature rising.

The captain straightened and turned to face me. 'Perhaps, Mrs Fisher, we should return later. You undoubtedly wish to return to your suite and prepare for the day. I believe you said you had to skip breakfast.'

I looked down at my grubby pyjamas.

'Yes, I suppose I should probably get dressed too.'

We left the still protesting Samuel Lawrence behind as the ever-gallant captain escorted me back to the Windsor Suite. There, my butler, Jermaine, was already laying out clothes for my day.

Today was going to be different to any since I had come aboard. I felt buoyant, light as a feather, and for the first time since I could remember, I had options. I was going to go shopping for new clothes, get a proper makeover in one of the many boutiques, and if I could do it without Barbie catching me, I was going to have a glass of champagne.

Reunited?

For the first time since I came on board, I woke up feeling relaxed. There was no longer a great weight hanging over my head. I was free and Commander Schooner was going to jail along with his goons. It was my fifth day on board and had been set to be my last.

Now, however, I had the option of staying on board to continue my trip and could bring Charlie on board with me. Yesterday afternoon, when I finally calmed down after the excitement of the morning, had time to eat and relax, and finally got my phone back, I called him.

Charlie sounded pleased to hear my voice and concerned that he hadn't heard from me for three days. I must report that he did manage to refrain from snapping at me when he pointed out that he had called me many, many times and left lots of messages both in text and voicemail form. It was the sort of short-tempered behaviour he might have displayed had he not recently been caught sleeping with my best friend. He was about as in the wrong as he could be.

I was polite on the phone though I avoided giving him all the details of recent events. I simply said I had not been able to fly home from Madeira and that I would be arriving in St Kitts in roughly eighteen hours where the ship was stopping for two days. My plan was still to leave the boat and fly home, but I still hadn't arranged a flight (because I had been afforded no opportunity to do so).

To my surprise, he claimed to have bought a ticket to St Kitts. He was actually getting on a flight. He was that desperate to see me and begin making amends.

I allowed him to apologise several more times before I grew bored of hearing it. In the end I snapped, 'If you are so sorry, Charlie, perhaps you should have considered the likely result of your actions before you decided to cheat.' I had never spoken to him like that in the thirty years we had been together.

It was clear that my tone surprised him from the silence at the other end.

'Yes, Patricia,' he said when he found his voice. 'I am sure I deserve that.'

'Yes,' I agreed. 'You do.'

'Patricia, you sound different,' he observed. I couldn't get that sentence out of my head for quite a while after the call ended.

I was different.

I felt different.

I was acting differently.

In the space of a week, well, less than a week actually, I had gone from bored, meek, and stifled middle-aged housewife with a job cleaning the homes of people with more interesting lives, to the woman staying in the best suite of the world's best cruise ship and I had money to spare.

On top of being given a refund for my around the world trip, I then discovered that the reward for the safe return of the sapphire was half a million US dollars. I almost fainted when the captain told me. Though I knew there were people on the planet who would consider it to be an insignificant sum, it was a fortune to me.

It took more than an hour before I came to my senses and insisted that the sum be split with Samuel Lawrence. Even though he was a slimy git, he had to be credited with bringing my attention to the jewel. Had it not been for him, I might never have worked it out. I also set aside a portion of the money for Jermaine and Barbie.

They both fought me and refused to accept it, but I insisted nevertheless, convincing them both that I would not feel comfortable keeping it all when I would be in a jail cell right now were it not for their efforts. Even giving away over half of the money, I still had more than enough.

I was rich.

I could get giddy thinking about it. Lying in bed, I stretched in place, wriggling around under the giant duvet while trying to make sense of all that had transpired in the last week. My life was somehow unrecognisable in comparison to what it had been. How much had I changed with it?

Last night, I paused in front of the mirror, wondering if I could detect a slimming around my waist. I told myself I was being ridiculous, but for the last week, my diet had been free of the usual processed foods I ate, water replaced alcohol and sugar-filled coffee, and I had actually exercised.

If a raised pulse helped to burn fat, then with all the drama and excitement I ought to have lost twenty pounds.

Thinking about it though, weight loss wasn't really the goal, it was a consequence. Yes, it wouldn't hurt to lose a few pounds, but I wasn't trying to please anyone but myself. Eating healthier food and drinking water since coming aboard were conscious choices, the result of which was a feeling of improved health. That was just diet though as opposed to dieting. I felt stronger and more confident, my inner strength - the thing Barbie constantly alluded to - was evident in every action.

With a smile because my life was turning a corner and that I would soon be reunited with an apologetic Charlie, I flung off the covers and went looking for my sports gear. I was going to go for a jog around the sun deck and I was genuinely looking forward to it.

Outside, the glorious early morning sun sparkled on the wave tips and a warm breeze ruffled my hair. It carried the scent of the sea and … hope? Hope was something I hadn't felt a few days ago. When I came on board, I felt despair. I had been lost, but though it sounded like a cliché, this had truly been a voyage of personal discovery.

I took ten laps of the sun deck, my pace slow but even. With each lap the mighty ship drew closer to the island ahead of us.

St Kitts - the sort of place I thought I would never visit. If I invited Charlie to join me on a free around the world cruise, would he do so? Would he enjoy it if he did? I frowned as I ran. Jermaine was in my suite right now packing my belongings back into my old, cheap suitcases.

On my ninth lap, I was starting to feel that I had done enough, and I was just about to pass the door that was closest to my suite when Barbie appeared. In her usual uniform of skin-tight Lycra, she looked as youthful and perfect as always. The only indication that she was a crew member was the badge pinned just above her right breast.

'Hi, Patty,' she waved a good morning.

I slowed and jogged in place. I was a little out of breath but managed to say, 'Good morning, Barbie.'

'I wondered if you wanted to weigh yourself this morning? We should chart your progress and it is obvious that you are losing weight.'

'Really?' I did feel thinner.

Barbie nodded with an encouraging smile. 'Shall we?'

I held up a finger, 'One more lap.'

She whooped in response as I set off around the sun deck again. The ship was almost in the dock, the process of coming alongside with such a huge vessel, a slow and deliberate thing.

Ten minutes later, Barbie escorted me into the gym where we repeated the process of measuring around my thighs and belly and other places. She used the callipers on my belly fat once more, making a note on a tablet as she did and then I stepped onto the scales.

I had lost eight pounds!

In just five days, I was eight pounds lighter. For the last two decades my weight had only moved in one direction. My past attempts to halt the process never lasted long. Over time I came to think of the pounds I dropped as not actually lost - more accurately they had gone away to fetch reinforcements.

As I stepped off the scales, I wrapped Barbie into a hug, saying, 'Thank you.' I was caught up in a feeling of elation that I was trying to quell. In that moment, I understood that losing weight or not was a choice I could make, but it wasn't something I had to do. Instead, what I needed was to find the beauty within myself and not allow the world to shackle me with a pattern I didn't fit. I was middle-aged and suddenly I was happy to be me, extra pounds or not.

As we parted, she asked, 'What are your plans for the day?'

'My husband is meeting me. He should be on the dock waiting for me when we arrive.'

Barbie's brow knitted in confusion. 'Your husband who cheated on you with your best friend?'

I nodded, sad and embarrassed by the truth of it. 'Yes, that one. He says he is sorry and just wants to go back to how things were.'

She pursed her lips, thinking. 'I know I have only known you for a few days, but you are a strong woman, Patty. I pushed you in the gym because I wanted to find your limit. You don't seem to have one. All the things you have done since you came on board: solving a thirty-year-old crime, solving the murders, and dealing with the accusations ... I couldn't have done that. It's not my place to say, but once a cheater, always a cheater and I feel that you deserve better.'

Barbie made some valid points, ones I had already partly acknowledged to myself. And her point about Charlie - I knew I had repeated the same cliché to other women at different points in the past and to myself this week. Was my Charlie any different? I was in St Kitts though and the two of us could spend the day talking and patching things up.

I had money, so I could do almost whatever I wanted. Perhaps today I would just be a tourist. There were guided trips the shipping line arranged which I overheard other passengers talking about last night. I could ask Jermaine about those.

With the weigh-in done, I wandered back to my suite in quiet reflection, my steps light though, as if there was now less holding me down. Of course, there was less holding me down, eight pounds less, but it wasn't just that. The old version of me was being replaced by a new one. My confidence was soaring, I felt strong and capable and for the first time in as long as I could remember, I felt excited to have options.

208

After breakfast I dressed in a new, short summer dress from a luxury boutique on the nineteenth deck, new strappy sandals, and a new wide-rimmed hat to keep off the sun. Since he chose to offer, I was allowing the captain to escort me down to the royal suites exit.

I wanted to look good when Charlie saw me and if he happened to catch a glimpse of me with a very good-looking man on my arm, then I doubted it would do any harm to make him jealous. I elected to leave my luggage in the suite for now and see what Charlie wanted to do. I saw no sense in taking my luggage down to the dock, as there was a chance he would agree to come on the cruise with me.

On the way down, the captain made polite conversation, this time telling me all about the Island of St Kitts, its history, the currency, the national bird. He could have been making most of it up for all I knew, but he was easy to listen to.

Too easy, in fact. He smelled good, he treated me like a lady and not a piece of furniture, and though it could be just his professional façade, I couldn't help but question whether I was getting something else.

I caught him looking my way more than once in the hours that followed the chase through the ship and Commander Schooner's flight from justice. He was looking at me and his expression was curious – it was like he was trying to decide something. He looked away each time I spotted him, pretending to be doing something else.

I did my best to not think about him – I already had too many confusing thoughts rampaging around my skull without adding the handsome captain into the mix.

The short passage that led from the elevators to the exit from the ship was filled with bright sunlight. The captain squinted against it as I fumbled in my bag for a pair of sunglasses. They were an old, cheap pair I had carried around for years. One of the arms was a little wonky. Looking at them, I decided it was time to buy a new pair. They would do for now though, so I slipped them on with my left hand as we reached the gangplank, since my right arm was still looped through the captain's.

Outside the ship, I had a spectacular view of the shore and the hotels that bordered it. Green hills stretched into the distance where the highest trees kissed the deep blue sky. At the bottom of the gangplank were uniformed security guards, but in contrast to the surly sneers I had received all week, both men were smiling as they bade me good morning and welcomed me to St Kitts.

Beyond them, lots of passengers were already ashore and mingling with the street sellers vending artisan textiles, paintings, and jewellery among other things. Were they always here ready to sell or did they see the great ships approaching on the horizon and run to meet them? Whatever the answer, they were pushy and determined and being held back by a barrier rope erected by the ship's crew. Charlie would be there somewhere, but I couldn't see him yet.

As I bid the captain a good day and set off toward the line of taxis behind the street vendors, he said, 'You won't need a taxi, Mrs Fisher. There is a limousine waiting to take you wherever you wish to go.' I looked at him in puzzlement. 'It's part of the royal suites package, Mrs Fisher. Have a good day.' Sure enough, a long, sleek, black limousine was gliding toward me along the dock.

Then, as a lady selling hats moved, her arms filled with them and held up for people to see, I spotted Charlie in the gap she left. He was looking right at me, but he didn't recognise the lady he was looking at. I was slimmer, I was more confident, and I was dressed very differently to my usual attire.

In that moment, looking at him and waiting for my heartrate to soar in elation, I realised nothing was happening. I was looking not at my husband, my dear beloved Charlie, but at a man that had done me harm. I should be feeling joy upon seeing him. The last five days were the longest we had been apart in the last thirty years, however, if anything, I felt disappointment.

I was disappointed to see him. If I went to him now, we would spend the day going over why he felt the need to cheat on me with my best friend, how he had ruined so many stable elements of my life, and how it was that we might hope to patch it up.

A man in the splendid white uniform of the Purple Star Cruise Lines stood poised to open the door of the black limousine for me. It was just a few feet away. I turned on my heel, smiling at the man as he swung the door open for me and I slid into the cool, airconditioned interior.

The driver looked up to make eye contact via his rear-view mirror, his darkly tanned face cleanly shaven except for a large, but well-trimmed moustache. 'Good morning, madam,' he said with a heavy Caribbean accent.

'Good morning,' I replied.

'Where would madam like to go, please?' He held an easy smile that made me believe he was utterly content in his life, something I felt was worth aiming for.

'I think perhaps, I would like to explore. Where can I get the best lobster on the island? Please take me there.'

He touched the brim of his chauffeur's peaked hat and pulled slowly away. I was leaving Charlie behind me in every sense of the word. There was a whole world waiting for me.

However, as I relaxed into the sumptuous leather, a chain of events I had unwittingly set in motion was conspiring to send me on an adventure that would change my life in ways I could never have imagined.

As for the sapphire ... well, that giant blue hunk of rock was on its way home, but I hadn't seen the last of it. Not by a long shot.

The End

(Except it isn't. This is just the beginning)

Author Note

Hello,

Thank you for reading my book. Without you, the reader, to give my characters life, they are but ideas in my head. Only when you absorb the words on the pages of my books do they truly exist, bursting into colour through your imagination.

The Missing Sapphire of Zangrabar is the first in what has become a long series. I wrote it while still in full time employment, but it became the catalyst to my exit from that life and the start of a dream becoming reality.

If you continue to read this series, you will come to know Patricia quite well. In the coming books, you can marvel as she throws off the shackles of her former life and blossoms to become the woman she was always meant to be.

Chances are that this is the first of my books you have ever read. That being the case, it may interest you to know that as at the time of writing this note, I have fifty-seven published works. They are listed in the pages that follow.

Over the last few years, I discovered my brand, which is to say I sat down and started writing to only later work out what kind of books I write. Almost exclusively, I write fast-paced mystery novels with action and adventure, risk, intrigue, and a dash of romance.

I like to write and have a head filled with stories clamouring to get out.

I live in the southeast corner of England in a small village surrounded by vineyards and spend my days tucked inside a log cabin at the bottom of my garden. I have two dachshunds, five chickens, two beautiful children, and a wife who smiles at me every day.

One thing I know for certain is there are lots more books to come and each will be as fast-paced and fun-filled as all the others.

Enjoy

Steve Higgs

What's Next for Patricia Fisher?

A cruise ship filled with gangsters, a missing woman, and a new head of security who can't do his job. What's a middle-aged sleuth to do?

Patricia just wants to spend more time in the company of Alistair Huntley, the offensively handsome captain of the Aurelia who seems only too happy to host her. But as the Aurelia sets sail from Miami, it does so with a dangerous new addition: there is a mob boss among the passengers and he's on the run – from more mobsters!

Any romantic notions are soon put aside when the mobster's reluctant-looking bride-to-be goes missing and Patricia is unexpectedly volunteered to solve the mystery of her disappearance. There's a cryptic ransom note where the missing woman should be and one of her bodyguards is soon found – with a hole in his head!

Regretting her decision to help out, it's not long before the opposing mobster factions take an interest in Patricia's involvement. Someone has the missing bride, everyone wants her, and they all think Patricia knows where she is.

With ever-faithful butler, Jermaine, at her side and perfect blonde, Barbie, to distract the men, Patricia will still have to go all out to unravel the riddle before anyone else turns up dead.

Where is the kidnapped bride? Find out for yourself as you take another hilarious, action-filled voyage with Patricia Fisher.

Books by Steve Higgs

Blue Moon Investigations

Paranormal Nonsense

The Phantom of Barker Mill

Amanda Harper Paranormal Detective

The Klowns of Kent

Dead Pirates of Cawsand

In the Doodoo With Voodoo

The Witches of East Malling

Crop Circles, Cows and Crazy Aliens

Whispers in the Rigging

Bloodlust Blonde – a short story

Paws of the Yeti

Under a Blue Moon – A Paranormal Detective Origin Story

Night Work

Lord Hale's Monster

The Herne Bay Howlers

Undead Incorporated

The Ghoul of Christmas Past

The Sandman

Jailhouse Golem

Shadow in the Mine

Patricia Fisher Cruise Mysteries

The Missing Sapphire of Zangrabar

The Kidnapped Bride

The Director's Cut

The Couple in Cabin 2124

Doctor Death

Murder on the Dancefloor

Mission for the Maharaja

A Sleuth and her Dachshund in Athens

The Maltese Parrot

No Place Like Home

Patricia Fisher Mystery Adventures

What Sam Knew

Solstice Goat

Recipe for Murder

A Banshee and a Bookshop

Diamonds, Dinner Jackets, and Death

Frozen Vengeance

Mug Shot

The Godmother

Murder is an Artform

Wonderful Weddings and Deadly Divorces

Dangerous Creatures

Patricia Fisher: Ship's Detective

Patricia Fisher: Ship's Detective

Albert Smith Culinary Capers

Pork Pie Pandemonium

Bakewell Tart Bludgeoning

Stilton Slaughter

Bedfordshire Clanger Calamity

Death of a Yorkshire Pudding

Cumberland Sausage Shocker

Arbroath Smokie Slaying

Dundee Cake Dispatch

Lancashire Hotpot Peril

Blackpool Rock Bloodshed

Felicity Philips Investigates

To Love and to Perish

Tying the Noose

Aisle Kill Him

Realm of False Gods

Untethered magic

Unleashed Magic

Early Shift

Damaged but Powerful

Demon Bound

Familiar Territory

The Armour of God

Made in the USA
Monee, IL
14 June 2023

35818489R00132